I0682381

BEAT
TO A
PULP

EDWARD A. GRAINGER'S
CASH LARAMIE & GIDEON MILES SERIES

as written by

WAYNE D. DUNDEE

This story first appeared in the short story collection *Trails of the Wild, Seven Tales of the Old West* published by BEAT to a PULP, 2013.

Cover images from iStock; Design by dMix.

ISBN: 978-0-9905916-4-1

BEAT to a PULP
PO Box 173
Freeville, New York 13068
USA
Email: btapzine@beattoapulp.com
Visit us at www.beattoapulp.com

Contents

Prologue 1

Chapter 1 7

Chapter 2 25

Chapter 3 33

Chapter 4 41

Chapter 5 51

Chapter 6 59

Chapter 7 67

Chapter 8 81

Chapter 9 91

Chapter 10 101

Chapter 11 113

Chapter 12 123

Chapter 13 133

Epilogue 141

About the Author 145

–PROLOGUE–

The rain and darkness made it difficult for Cash to spot the sentry. In fact, he was almost on the verge of concluding that, because of the storm, the gang had decided not to post a lookout in the belief that no one was likely to be closing in on them under these conditions.

If they figured that, then they weren't reckoning on the tenacity of U.S. Deputy Marshal Cash Laramie.

At that moment, a rolling flicker of lightning coming quick on the heels of a low growl of thunder, reflected for the briefest second off the shift of a rifle barrel in some underbrush only a dozen or so yards ahead of where Cash knelt.

Cash backhanded rainwater away from his face and smiled grimly. With the lookout's position fixed firmly in his bearings now, he began to edge forward and slightly to the right. He moved in a low prowl, the barrel of his own Winchester Yellowboy pressed tight to his body, under the fall of his dull charcoal-colored slicker, so no sudden lightning pop could betray him in the same manner as the sentry.

The sound of his movement was effectively muffled by the steady hiss of the falling rain and the low moan of the wind, not to mention the intermittent thunder.

Even without these aids, however, Cash was highly skilled—thanks to the training he had gotten during his formative years being raised by a band of Arapaho—in the art of silently stalking prey.

As even the most fleeting memory of those years often did, tonight it caused Cash to reach involuntarily with his free hand and touch the arrowhead that hung around his neck on a leather thong. The arrowhead had been a gift from his dying Arapaho mother and he was never without it. Touching the simple talisman, no matter if done without conscious thought or awareness, somehow soothed and seemed to provide a measure of reassurance in the face of any situation.

Cash circled around to the rear of the lookout's position and then moved up behind him. Since making the costly mistake that gave away his position, the man had remained very still. But it was too late.

Gripping his Winchester in both hands—one near the end of the barrel, the other just behind the cocking lever—Cash leaned in close enough to smell the unwashed sourness of the man, even through the dousing rain. Bracing himself, he raised the Winchester up above the man's head and then lunged forward, sweeping the rifle down over the sentry's face and jerking back hard against his throat. Cash felt the windpipe collapse, heard the crunch of the larynx. The victim struggled briefly, one foot kicking in and out, hands clawing at the rifle, trying to pry it away. But it was all in vain. Soon his body sagged limp and still.

Cash let the body slip to the ground, and then he dropped into a motionless crouch, listening intently, eyes slitted against the brilliance of the lighting pops while taking in as much as he could during those brief moments of illumination.

Satisfied the brief struggle had not been heard and was not generating any response, Cash rose up and stepped forward over the fallen body. He didn't know which member of the Driscoll gang he had just killed, but it really didn't matter. Unless, of course, it was Everett Driscoll himself. The elimination of their leader would have devastated the other gang members and made the rest of Cash's job a lot easier ... but that was too much to hope for. No way Everett was even-handed enough to assign himself sentry duty, especially not on a night like this.

Cash stepped out of the underbrush, out into the open and the rain again, and began making his way upslope toward the mouth of the shallow cave where the remaining four members of the gang were holed up for the night. He allowed himself neither remorse nor regret over the one he'd killed. Leaving the man alive—even unconscious and restrained, if he'd taken the time—was too much of a risk to have that close behind him while he went to deal with the others. Furthermore, there wasn't a member of the gang who hadn't proven many times over to be evil and bloodthirsty enough to deserve killing.

At the top of the slope, Cash paused to one side of the cave's narrow opening. Off to his left, where he had determined some time earlier the horses were staked, he heard one of the animals chuff. From inside the cave came so much ragged snoring it was a marvel any of those present could sleep a wink. And overhead, thunder growled regularly.

Cash smiled his grim smile again. Christ, with so much other noise drowning out his approach, it almost seemed like he could have thrown caution to the wind and marched in tooting a bugle and beating a drum. But approaching a potentially dangerous situation with caution was too ingrained in Cash, too much a part of him, to ever change. It was what had kept him alive this long in a profession where anything less could be permanently career and life ending.

Timing it not to be backlit by a burst of lightning while he was framed in the opening, Cash glided ghostlike into the cave and flattened himself against the rocky wall amidst a pool of dense shadows. The interior was predominantly dark and shadow-filled, but the softly glowing coals of a nearly dead fire gave off a faint reddish light.

As Cash's eyes adjusted, he could make out the four shapes of as many sleeping men. In the confined space, their snores were even louder. But outside the storm was intensifying, the accelerated claps of thunder and increasing howl of the wind doing their share to maintain command over the sounds of the night. Cash knew the gang members were weary, having ridden long and hard to try and stay ahead of him. So he expected their slumber to remain deep. But at the same time he wanted to make sure he took advantage while that was still the case.

Again moving ghostlike, Cash advanced on the glowing coals and picked up a pair of medium-sized branches from the nearby pile of firewood. He laid these carefully across the coals and then stepped back, pausing to make certain his movement hadn't disturbed anyone. When he was confident it hadn't, he moved again, this time to seize up three rifles and one discarded gun belt he spotted lying outside the bedrolls of the sleeping gang members. He knew there was bound to be more weapons *inside* the bedrolls, but getting rid of these would be a start. He carried the confiscated guns over to the cave opening and flung them out into the stormy night.

Then he stayed there, standing just within the cave's entrance, giving him the widest vantage point over both the interior and the sleeping men. When the time was right, he wanted everything and everybody well lighted and well within his range of vision. Quietly, he pulled four sets of handcuffs from a slicker pocket and let them dangle from his free hand, making sure the chains were not tangled.

The freshly-applied branches started to hiss and then crackle and then the first tiny flames started to lick up out of the coals. Cash waited with the patience of an Arapaho hunter.

Behind him, outside, the storm continued to grow stronger. Pitchforks of lightning stabbed the boiling sky, thunder crashed almost constantly, and the rain came down harder, blowing against his back and skimming across the hinges of his jaw. Rivulets of rainwater were now gushing down from the rim of the high, rocky cliff into whose face the cave opening was notched.

Cash flipped up the slicker's collar and continued to wait. The branches were starting to burn stronger and the interior of the cave was growing brighter. Another minute or two and the time would be right to roust this pack of rattlers, shoot any of them who weren't smart enough to see he had control over the situation, and then—

Without warning, a fat section of rock and mud and gravel tore away with a great growling, sucking sound from the cliff face directly above the cave opening where Cash stood. It tumbled down and partially into the notch right on top of him. Cash had no chance to react. He heard the strange noise and felt the crushing weight all in the same instant. The top of his head exploded with pain as a heavy rock within the falling mass slammed against his skull and when he opened his mouth to cry out it filled with mud and gravel. Then his ears filled, too, and the only sound he could hear after that was the scream coming from inside him.

–1–

Four riders sat their horses on the crown of a low hill overlooking a shallow valley. Down on the valley floor, the yellow-tinted lights of a small town were starting to blink on like swarming fireflies. The sun was less than an hour set and soon the rising moon and a blanket of stars in the cloudless sky would cast a bluish silver contrast to the pale gold of the town's lamps and lanterns.

"Well, there she sits, boys," drawled Everett Driscoll. "Yuba City—as fresh and innocent as a honeymoon bride, waitin' for us to come along and pluck her cherry."

The horsemen on either side of him guffawed obligingly.

Everett was a big, heavy-gutted man with weathered lines around his eyes and a puckered scar on his left cheek, partially covered by curly whiskers shot with flecks of gray. He cut his eyes over to the rider on his left, the youngest of the bunch. "How about it, kid? You ready to play your part?"

When Vint Brenner responded, his tone didn't sound quite as confident as his words. "Hell yeah, I'm ready. Can't hardly wait."

Everett eyed him. "Sure you ain't nervous?"

The kid—lean and handsome, clean-shaven, with dark hair and intelligent eyes set off by a glint of recklessness—managed a smile. But it, too, seemed a little uncertain. "If I am, it's only from being too close to this damn thing." He reached up and tapped the U.S. deputy marshal's badge worn on the front of his shirt. "I been too long on the dodge from anybody packin' one of these. I'm afraid havin' it pinned right next to my skin might cause my poor old unaccustomed body to break out in hives or boils or something."

Everett threw back his head and brayed with laughter. The other two men—Everett's brother Clem, and their cousin Burt Ketchel—joined in and stayed with it until Vint thought they sounded like three jackasses carrying on. He let his uncertain smile stay in place, but he didn't see where what he'd said had been so damn funny.

"Whoee, that was a good one," Everett gasped when he was finally done laughing. "Boy, I been runnin' from jaspers wearin' badges for more years than you been alive. If bein' too long on the dodge was cause enough for a body to break out in hives if'n they ever *did* get close to a badge, then I would be one big-ass pile of leaking sores right about now from just riding beside you."

"Same goes for the rest of us," Clem allowed. He was three years older than Everett, narrow-shouldered but also carrying too much gut, with eyes set too close above a pointy little nose and a scraggly walrus mustache. "Havin' that badge ain't nothing to be nervous or scared over. Not at all. Fact is, gettin' our hands on that piece of tin and then Everett comin' up with a plan on how to put it to use along with the other stuff we took off that law dog's body, well it could turn out to be the best stroke of luck we ever run across."

No sooner had he spoken those final words than Clem frowned, his expression looking like he'd bitten into something with an awful taste. He cut his eyes anxiously over to Burt Ketchel. "Aw, hell, Burt," he said. "I'm sorry for the way that might've sounded. I sure didn't mean that losin' your brother—not that part of it—was any kind of good luck."

Ketchel, a tall, gangly, towheaded specimen with a grotesquely large nose and a bobbing lump of an Adam's apple almost as big, returned Clem's anxious gaze with sad, earnest eyes. "That's all right, Clem," he replied, his voice a surprisingly deep rumble from within his scrawny neck. "I know you didn't mean it that way."

Brusquely, Everett said, "Okay. Now that we've made sure nobody's tender feelings have been bruised and the kid here has given us all a good laugh, it's time to get down to the business that brought us here."

He reached back into his saddlebags and withdrew a pair of handcuffs that he clamped onto his wrists, giving the appearance that his arms were fastened together in front of him. In truth, however, the cuffs had been carefully filed so that the locking prongs slid into place with a realistic click and even provided a bit of resistance when tugged at. But only a minimal amount. When jerked forcefully, the cuffs would pop open every time.

Clem and Burt each produced their own pair of cuffs and clamped them on. Theirs had been rigged the same as Everett's. Meanwhile, Vint climbed down from his saddle and tied the reins of the three men's horses together so that no single animal could break free and gallop away from of the rest. Then he swung back up onto his own mount.

"Okay, that should do it," Everett announced. "Time to take your prisoners on into town now, Vint-boy." Then, his mouth tilting into a lopsided grin, he added, "Excuse me … I mean, Marshal Laramie."

* * *

"Sure sorry to drag you away from the supper table like I done, Sheriff," Vint Brenner was saying. "I was aiming to make it to town before sundown. But I guess I don't have to tell you that the country hereabouts can be a mite rugged. And it goes without sayin' that these hombres I'm herdin' weren't being overly cooperative."

"Don't you worry about it. Not one bit," replied Tom Weatherby, the sheriff of Yuba City. He was a bespectacled middle-aged man, average-sized, with bushy gray sideburns and a good start on a pot belly. "Any time I can lend a hand puttin' Everett Driscoll and his bloodthirsty pack behind bars—not to mention bein' a service to you, Marshal Laramie—ain't something I consider any kind of inconvenience. It's a damn pleasure!"

Vint was finally starting to relax. In fact, he felt downright calm. It was all he could do to keep a wide, smug smile from spreading across his face. But that, of course, would never do. It not only would run the risk of raising Sheriff Weatherby's suspicions, but acting too cocky was bound to earn the wrath of Everett later on.

Still, it was mighty damn slick how they were pulling this off. How *he* was successfully passing himself as Cash Laramie.

When Everett had first suggested the idea—after they'd partially dug the limp, crushed body of the real Laramie out from under the mud and rock slide and stripped it of its gun and badge and the rest, including locating the marshal's big pinto stallion staked nearby that stormy night—it sounded plumb loco. Leastways, it sure as hell had to Vint, who was the one tagged to take on the marshal's identity because he bore such a close resemblance.

The others took to the notion quick enough, but Vint wasn't so fast to buy in. Although he eventually had to pretend to be sold on it (after all, it wasn't smart to show too much resistance to one of Everett's ideas), he'd remained unsure right up to the minute they arrived at Weatherby's house, interrupting his supper, and the sheriff took to calling him "Marshal Laramie" without hesitation.

The sheriff was equally receptive to Vint's well-practiced spiel about capturing what was left of the notorious Driscoll gang—having had to dispatch two of them in the process, he'd explained—and needing a lock-up to hold them overnight so he could get some much-needed rest before continuing on with them to

Cheyenne. Weatherby was all too willing to make a couple of his jail cells available, and even offered to provide a deputy to stand overnight guard on the outlaws so Vint could catch some proper sleep in a soft hotel room bed.

They were on their way to the jail now. Weatherby was walking along beside the horses, pointing the way, jabbering excitedly as they proceeded down the dusty street. Vint was mounted on Paint, the real Laramie's confiscated pinto, riding behind the still-handcuffed Everett and the others, wielding a shotgun to maintain the appearance of being ready to mow them down if they tried anything funny.

When they reached the sheriff's office and jail, Weatherby's deputy—a young fellow he called Sweeney—was there waiting for them. Weatherby had arranged for this by calling out a patron from inside a saloon they were passing and sending the man to fetch Sweeney, who was out making rounds.

"Got your message, Sheriff," Sweeney said now, by way of greeting. "I ran ahead and made sure the cells were ready and everything."

The lad gave the impression of being fairly new to the job, obviously green, eager as all hell to please.

Weatherby nodded approvingly. "Good. Now tie those horses to the hitch rail there and then go inside and stand ready while the marshal brings his prisoners in. Stay out of the way unless he asks something specific of you."

"Yes, sir."

Vint dismounted and then Everett, Clem, and Burt

climbed down, their cuffs and chains rattling convincingly. Vint moved in close behind them, still brandishing the shotgun, and herded them into the jail. Weatherby, who had taken time to strap on a gun belt before leaving his house, walked at the fake marshal's side with his hand resting on the grip of his revolver. As soon as they were inside, Vint heeled the heavy door shut behind them.

"I'd suggest putting 'em two to a cell. Right back there," the sheriff said.

Vint nodded. "Good idea, sheriff … except for one thing."

"What's that?"

"This!" Vint said, pivoting and driving the butt of his shotgun hard and deep into the sheriff's gut. Weatherby emitted a wet gagging sound as he doubled sharply forward and sagged at the knees.

On the other side of the room, Deputy Sweeney took a step and blurted "Sheriff!" without even thinking to reach for the pistol holstered at his hip. As the prisoners shuffled in, Everett, the strongest member of the gang, had positioned himself nearest Sweeney. Now, popping the modified handcuff restraints with a single outward jerk of his arms, he let the movement carry him halfway around so that he blocked the startled lunge of the deputy. The young man's momentum carried him straight into Everett's waiting fists and the flurry of clubbing blows they eagerly delivered. Sweeney was driven back and down, knocked unconscious before he ever fully comprehended what was happening.

It was over as suddenly as it started. For a long

second, the only sounds in the room were the tick of a clock on the wall and the low groans leaking out of Weatherby.

Then Everett turned back to face the others, a wide, rake-hell grin splitting the lower half of his face. "Didn't I tell you it would work slick as bear grease? Didn't I?" His eyes shone with excitement. "And you, Vint-boy, you did terrific! Holy shit, kid, you were so convincing you almost had *me* ready to believe you were Cash Laramie."

Clem and Burt joined in agreement and praise. Vint flushed with embarrassment, but was pleased to hear it all the same.

"Hang on, though. Let's not get too full of ourselves," Everett cautioned, his grin fading. "The job is only part way done, remember."

The others turned sober-faced as well.

Everett started snapping off orders. "Clem, find something to gag and hogtie this stringbean of a deputy, then drag him over and lock him in one of them cells … Burt, help me get the sheriff back on his feet so's he can start to catch his breath and get his mind right for what's gonna come next and what more we'll be needin' from him if he wants to see the rest of it go with nobody gettin' serious hurt … Vint, you keep your eyes peeled to make sure nothing is stirring out in the street."

* * *

"This is rather unusual, no doubt about it," Mordecai Croft commented for the third or fourth time as he fussed with the ring of keys to unlock the rear door of the Pioneer First Bank & Trust, where he presided as president. "But anything I can do to assist in the capture and incarceration of the Driscoll gang is purely my pleasure. What's more, you can't imagine how much relief and peace of mind it will bring—no longer having to worry that *my* bank might be the next one in line for those ruthless dogs to hit."

Croft got the door open and led the way into the rear office area of the bank where he promptly lighted a pair of lanterns and adjusted them to full illumination. He turned to the three men who had entered with him—a sullen, pinch-faced Sheriff Weatherby along with Vint and Everett, whom the sheriff had introduced, respectively, as "Federal Marshal Cash Laramie and his deputy."

The sheriff had shown up at Croft's house, accompanied by the two fake lawmen, a short time earlier. Another supper interrupted, another request made by the renowned "Cash Laramie" to impose on the bank president in the guise of aiding law and order.

Croft handed one of the lanterns to Weatherby. "How much money did you say was in there?" he asked, tipping his head to indicate the satchel Everett was carrying.

The bank president was a tall man, solid-looking across the chest and shoulders, but with a weak chin and a pale, doughy face framed by skull-tight, slicked-down black hair.

"Reckon the sheriff don't know the answer to that," Vint was quick to reply, aiming a disarming smile at Croft after first slicing a hard-eyed warning glance in

Weatherby's direction. The sheriff was managing to follow the instructions he'd been given, but wasn't doing a very good job of masking his reluctance and bitterness toward the situation. Vint was concerned his ill-concealed true feelings might show through to a point where he'd cause Croft to start smelling something fishy.

"You see," Vint continued, "the sheriff don't know how much is in that satchel because I never told him. Truth to tell, I don't know myself. I never got around to counting it."

Croft's eyebrows went up. "That makes you an even more amazing man than I've heard, Marshal Laramie. Very few individuals would have the willpower to resist examining the contents of that bag if they suspected it contained a significant amount."

Vint shrugged. "I don't know about that. All I know is that I haven't had a lot of time for counting, not since we took those Driscoll scoundrels *and* the bag into custody. But according to the posse members who rode with me and my deputy until they petered out and turned back, Driscoll and his bunch made off with over fifty grand from the Hopperville bank. Since we've been steppin' on their tails practically from the first, I don't see where they had much chance to get rid of any of it."

The dollar signs practically danced in Croft's eyes. "You mean you expect fifty thousand or more to still be in there?"

While Croft was staring greedily at the satchel, Vint glanced again at Weatherby. Everett had stepped up close behind him and was hovering there in a silently menacing manner. The sheriff continued to look a little chalky-faced and nervous, but was fighting hard to put up a passable front.

Returning his attention to Croft, Vint said, "If that was the true start figure, then I guess I do. You can see why I'd like to have it locked away safe and secure in your bank vault overnight. With the sheriff here agreeing to hold our prisoners behind bars in his jail, and the money now in the capable hands of you and your bank—well, that'd give me and my deputy our first chance in quite a spell to catch a peaceful night's sleep. Can't tell you how grateful we'd be. Then, come tomorrow, we'll move on with our prisoners and the money and be out of your hair."

"Believe me, for reasons already stated, the gratitude would certainly cut both ways," Croft assured him. "Isn't that right, Sheriff?"

"Right," Weatherby muttered tersely.

Croft beamed a wide smile. "Enough talk, then. Let's find a spot to bed down that money so you gentlemen can seek out the same and get the peaceful night's sleep you so richly deserve."

Croft led the way deeper into the bank, passing behind a row of teller cages then over to a large vault sunken into an inner wall. The flickering lantern light cast shifting, often grotesquely shaped shadows as they moved along. Vint was glad to see that heavy shades had been pulled down over the westward-facing front windows.

Reaching the vault, Croft announced, "Rest assured,

the Hopperville money will be quite secure here until you are ready to reclaim it tomorrow."

There was a moment of awkward hesitation as—without wanting to make the precaution appear too obvious—the bank president positioned his body in a manner meant to make sure the others were blocked from seeing the numbers he spun to open the combination lock on the vault door. Once the act was achieved, however, it took only a few seconds of whirring clicks before the heavy door was unlocked and Croft gave a tug on the latching lever to pull it open. Lantern light spilled in to reveal the neat rows of safety deposit boxes, trays of coins, and tidy stacks of paper money.

Everett spoke for the first time, saying, "You're pretty cocky about havin' a real secure set-up here, ain't you?"

Croft's scowl indicated he was somewhat offended by the tone of the question. "Most assuredly, sir."

"Well then," Everett drawled, reaching for his Colt in a smooth, almost casual manner, "how do you explain us bein' here to rob the joint and you standin' there holdin' the door wide open to accommodate us?"

Croft's expression melted into one of confusion and then alarm. His eyes shot first to Vint for an answer, but all he got in return was the sight of the masquerading marshal drawing the Colt and aiming it at him underneath a taunting smile.

When the bank man's gaze went to Weatherby, the sheriff's expression was one of pain and regret. "They got us cold, Mordecai," he said dully. "The Driscoll gang is in town right enough. Trouble is, they ain't behind bars in my jail. Part of 'em's standing right here before you—including Everett himself and the young pup pretending to be a federal marshal."

Croft looked stunned. "But how can that be? We've all heard descriptions of Cash Laramie … The arrowhead talisman he wears around his neck, the big pinto stallion like the one outside. To say nothing of the badge! I don't understand—"

"I don't know the whole of it," Weatherby interrupted him. "But what I do know is that another gang member has got Sweeney under the gun back at the jail and still another has gone to my house with orders to blast my wife at the first sign of trouble if I don't cooperate fully."

"And that's all anybody *needs* to know," Everett said harshly. "Was a time—and not so very long ago, as you're both damn well aware—me and my boys would have ridden into this piss puddle of a town, shot everything and everybody to hell, picked your bank clean and left a pile of dead bodies in our wake as we rode away. What we're trying here is a less rowdy way to go about it. You could say I'm startin' to tame down in my old age. Oh, you and your gobs of precious money will still end up parting ways, banker man, but as long as everybody is willing to cooperate—like the sheriff is smart enough to see—it can be done without all the shootin' and killin'."

"Says you," Croft sneered.

"Damned right, says me," Everett snarled right back. "And as long as me and my boys are the ones who've got the bulge on this thing, what I say is all that really matters."

"For Christ's sake, Mordecai, do as he says," Weatherby urged. "Didn't you hear what I said before? They've threatened to kill my Mary if there's any resistance. They know where you live, too. What makes you think your wife is any safer?"

Croft's face turned purple. "Why don't you put ideas in their heads, you cowering fool?"

"Knock it off, the both of you! You want to go at each other's throats, we'll be happy to lock you in the vault before we ride away and whoever finds you in the morning can decide who came out on top … if we leave you alive at all, that is!" Everett took the lantern from Croft and shoved the satchel at him. "Dump out the wadded newspaper and adobe bricks we stuffed in there—that's the big haul you've been drooling over, banker man. Then start replacing it with what's gonna be our *real* haul. I'll tell you when you got it full enough."

Vint motioned with his gun to get Weatherby's attention, then held out his free hand for the other lantern. "You better do the money-handlin', Sheriff. Mr. Banker might up and have a stroke on us if he has to be the one to actually fork over his precious bills."

"You have no worry as far as me having a stroke," Croft said through clenched teeth. "I have every intention of living long enough to one day see you thieving bastards hang!"

Sighing wearily, Everett reached out and calmly placed his lantern on a narrow shelf jutting out from the wall near where he stood. Then, with savage suddenness, he wheeled back and slammed the long barrel of his Colt to the side of Croft's face. The banker staggered away from the blow, arms flailing in an attempt to catch his balance. All he succeeded in doing was to upend one of the coin trays as he went down. He sprawled to the floor with coins spilling all around him and a bright red welt forming over his shattered cheekbone.

"Goddamn you!" Everett bellowed. "I told you we were trying to do this without the rough stuff. But that don't mean I *won't* resort to the old ways if you push me too far. You've done opened the vault, you dumb bastard. You lost the one sliver of an edge you might've had. Blowin' your brains out now won't cost me a damn thing but the price of a bullet."

"Don't shoot him. Don't kill him," Weatherby pleaded. "He'll cooperate from here out. I'll see to it he does."

The sheriff leaned over to give Croft a hand back to his feet.

"Leave him!" Everett ordered. "He put himself there, he can haul his own ass back up. And he'd better make it quick 'cause he's wore my patience about as thin as I'll allow."

Weatherby straightened back up. His eyes bounced back and forth the outlaw and the fallen man.

Croft, who had sprawled face down, put his palms flat on the floor and lifted his upper body, at the same time rolling onto his left hip. He groaned faintly, either from the effort or from the pain of his broken cheekbone that was inflamed and already beginning to swell.

"Come on. Move it. We ain't got all damn night!" barked Everett. "Didn't you hear me say I've about run out of—"

Suddenly, Croft gave a hard push with both hands. He rolled the rest of the way over onto his rump and leaned into an upright sitting position. At the same time, his right hand flashed across his chest and reached inside the left lapel of his coat. It jerked out a second later gripping a large bore over/under derringer.

"No!" Sheriff Weatherby tried to protest.

But it was too late to stop what Croft had set in motion.

The sheer boldness of his move—going for the derringer with two guns already drawn against him—damn near bought him enough time to get off at least one shot. But not quite. The unexpectedness of his desperate act froze Everett and Vint only a fraction of a second before their Colts roared simultaneously, spitting lead and clouds of rolling blue smoke. Four slugs ripped into the banker, knocking him back down from his sitting position and hammering him to the floor. The derringer flew from his hand and went skittering across the spilled coins as they were simultaneously painted with gushing blood.

Weatherby threw up his hands and cringed back against the stacks of bundled money. "Not me! Don't shoot me, I didn't do anything," he wailed.

"Well," said Everett, re-adjusting his aim. "Then maybe you should have, you lily-livered puke." And he emptied the rest of his cylinder on the sheriff.

Watching Weatherby's limp body slide slowly down to the floor, Vint matter-of-factly observed, "He's gettin' blood on some of the money."

"It'll still spend, don't worry about it," Everett replied as he punched the spent shells from his gun and began reloading. "Start stuffing that satchel. Pick around the bloody bills as best you can."

–2–

Emerging from his bedroll under the lead wagon, Frank Wizarious—better known throughout eastern Wyoming, western Nebraska, and parts of South Dakota as "Professor" Wizarious of the Wizarious Wonder Tonic Extravaganza—was immediately drawn by the welcome aroma of freshly brewed coffee. The scent wafted from a pot perched on the coals at the edge of a small fire crackling in the center of the camp.

Hitching up his suspenders and stamping his feet a couple more times to better secure the fit of his boots, Wizarious wasted no time heading straight for the pot. He was a tall, lanky man in his late forties with a purposeful stride and alert, intelligent eyes beneath a ledge of bristly, gray-shot brows and a headful of equally bristly brown hair also shot through with streaks of gray. His lankiness might have been mistaken for sparse physical strength if one failed to note the thickness of his wrists or the solid, rolling balance in the way he carried his long frame. Still, given that he was frequently seen in the company of the show's heavily-muscled strongman, he generally came across as looking scrawny, even to the most discerning eye.

An attractive young woman sat on a folding chair beside the fire, a cup of the pot's contents already in hand. She looked up at the sound of Wizarious' approach and greeted him with a bright smile. "Good morning, Uncle."

"Good morning indeed," he responded. Then, rummaging a tin cup from the box of eating utensils that sat on the ground nearby, he added, "Made all the more so, it appears, by an early spurt of ambition and domesticity on your part."

Seizing the coffee pot with the aid of a leather glove to shield against the heat of the handle, Beatrice Hale—who performed in her uncle's show as Beatrice Blaze, songstress and trick shot artist—poured some of the steaming brew into the cup Wizarious held out. "Much as I'd like to take credit for this 'spurt of domesticity,' as you put it," she said, "I'm afraid I cannot. You see, I rose only a few minutes ago myself. All of this was already completed—thanks to our new traveling companion."

"You mean Smitty?"

Beatrice topped off her own cup and then returned the pot to the coals. "I guess that's what you've taken to calling him. He doesn't seem to mind."

"No, he doesn't. In fact, like everything else we've done to accommodate him—and none of it has been all that extraordinary, I dare say—he seems deeply grateful. And, you've got to admit, being called 'Smitty' rather than 'Hey, you' would be preferable to most people."

"I suppose," Beatrice conceded.

"Where is he, by the way?"

Beatrice made a non-specific motion with her hand.

"He went off to gather some more firewood and fetch water to fill the water barrel on the wagon."

After taking a sip from his cup, Wizarious commented admiringly, "He not only is an industrious fellow, he makes a damn fine pot of coffee."

"True. The only skills he seems to be lacking are in the memory department when it comes to his identity and whatever events brought on the predicament in which we found him."

"You continue to be suspicious of him, don't you?"

"I don't really want to be," Beatrice said, giving a faint head shake that caused her spill of long, pale gold hair to shimmer in the early morning light. "But I can't help it. What's more, I'm surprised that neither you nor Theron aren't equally so—especially Theron, who seldom trusts anybody about anything."

The object of that observation, Theron Tolos, a powerful Greek giant who'd made his way west all the way from New York City and now played his part in the Wizarious Extravaganza as the Hercules of the High Plains, was still asleep in his bedroll under the second wagon. Growing up in one of the city's roughest neighborhoods had made him guarded and mistrustful at an early age and neither were traits he was ready to give up, even though in the company of those he knew and felt comfortable with, he was the first to crack a joke or rumble with hearty laughter.

"But when he makes up his mind, Theron has a keen sense for reading people," Wizarious pointed out. "Maybe you'd do well to consider that *he* has relaxed his suspicion where Smitty is concerned."

Beatrice scowled, failing to look convinced.

"The man was nearly dead when we happened on him, drawn by the circling vultures," Wizarious went on. "The blows he suffered to the head and body from that rockslide he was practically buried under *would* have killed a lesser man. He was unconscious for three days and has now been up and about for only two. It's amazing he's functioning as well as he is. Why is it so hard to accept he came out of all that a bit muddled and disoriented?"

Beatrice's brilliant blue eyes flashed. "Because it seems too darn *convenient*, that's why."

"I don't even know what that is supposed to mean."

"It means what about the other things we spotted where we found him? The fresh grave nearby, the signs of several men and horses having stayed there in that cave whose opening was almost covered by the same rockslide that caught him? Why did they just ride away and leave him that way?"

"Obviously, they left him for dead."

"So they took time to bury one man, but not another? What does that tell you?"

"Maybe Smitty came along *after* the other men had left and was unfortunate enough to get caught by that rockslide when there was no one else around."

"So it was the rockslide that stripped him of his guns and hat and every scrap of identity? And what became of his horse?"

"After its rider was unresponsive for a long enough time, is it so surprising the horse might wander off? And not every man carries a handgun holstered on his hip, you know. There are such things as rifles and you usually find them in a saddle boot, which could be where Smitty left his when he went to check that cave." Wizarious shrugged. "Horse wanders off, gun wanders off with it."

"You've got all the answers, don't you?" Beatrice's tone was annoyed, but not really angry.

Her uncle smiled tolerantly. "I have some possible explanations, that's all. Ones that might make our Smitty something other than the mysterious desperado you seem to want to conjure up. There is a growing acceptance of a medical condition, for instance, called amnesia that can affect a person's memory after a shock to the system such as Smitty suffered."

"Then why have you been so reluctant to take him to a doctor?"

"Mainly because I doubt any of the doctors in these small communities out here on the frontier have sufficient knowledge or experience to be of much use treating—or even verifying—such a condition. Also, there is the matter of Smitty's privacy. Considering the circumstances in which we found him, I think it best *he* makes the decision on just how much he wants to solicit input from others."

Beatrice seized on this admission. "Aha! So I'm not the only one 'conjuring up' suspicions that his past might be somewhat checkered."

"No, but you're the only one who's already convinced yourself—and pre-convicted him, I might add—of that mere possibility."

"I'm simply making observations and attempting to

draw some conclusions from them."

"Okay. How about if I've got an observation that you apparently missed?"

"Such as?"

"Remember the shirt Smitty was wearing when we found him? I asked you to wash it and see if there was any use left in it so he'd have something to put on when he regained consciousness?"

"It was nothing but rags. So torn and battered from the rockslide that it was useless as far as ever being worn again."

"Agreed. But before you tossed it in the rag bin, I noticed something. On the left side of the shirt's front, in the area just above the breast pocket, there was a spot of bright color that wasn't as faded from exposure as the rest of the shirt ... it was the size and roughly the shape of a typical lawman's badge. A marshal, say, or maybe a sheriff."

"Are you saying you think our Smitty may be a law officer of some kind?"

Wizarious shrugged again. "All I'm saying is if the shirt he was wearing belonged to him for any length of time—in other words, if he didn't buy it used or something—then the wear pattern on it looked to me like *somebody* who wore it also wore some kind of badge." Another flash of the tolerant smile. "That may not make Smitty as exciting as a desperado on the run, but I think it's a reasonable alternative at least worth considering. It also could fit with some of those curious things you mentioned about how and where we found him, and provides reason enough to continue giving him the benefit of the doubt while he's trying to get things sorted out in his head."

Beatrice's shoulders slumped. "Now I feel foolish."

"Nonsense," Wizarious told her. "Your suspicions may yet prove to have merit. Better to err on the side of caution than negligence. In the meantime, we'll continue to allow Smitty to travel with us while he's recuperating. During that time, we naturally will keep a close eye on him, but we'll do so with an open mind."

–3–

The following day, just before noon on another sunny spring morning, the Wizarious Wonder Tonic Extravaganza arrived in the western Nebraska town of Corryton. Judging from the interest and excitement shown by the locals as they emerged from their homes and businesses to watch the wagons come rolling in, the turnout for that evening's performance held promise of being a good one.

After checking in with the town marshal, Wizarious was granted permission to park their wagons and set up their tents on the north end of town in a grassy meadow ringed by a fringe of cottonwood trees.

The passage through the town was done, as usual, with everyone decked out in full costume. The wagons were halted at frequent intervals so the performers could preview a snippet of the routines that would be done in their entirety during the complete show later on.

Beatrice, in her guise as "Beatrice Blaze: The Queen of Ballads and Bullets," stood atop the gaudily painted lead wagon, spinning her gleaming pistols and firing blank shots in the air with special smoke charges for added effect. From the seat of the lead wagon, Wizarious, having now donned his role as Professor Wizarious, did sleight of hand tricks with collapsing wands and disappearing handkerchiefs. Following in the second wagon, Theron Tolos, the Greek giant with muscles that bulged like a young mountain range, would normally have played his part from the wagon seat also; but with Smitty present to handle the team of matched pure white horses, identical to those pulling the lead wagon, he was able to climb atop the wagon and perform a series of poses and exercises that displayed his amazing muscularity to a jaw-dropping response from the onlookers.

By the time they reached the appointed meadow, the crowd they'd drawn was dispersing in their wake as the townsfolk returned to their normal daily duties and activities. The one exception was a gaggle of young boys who followed the wagons into the meadow and awaited the handfuls of fliers they knew from past experience would be available to distribute and post for modest payment.

Professor Wizarious took care of this latter bit of business, cheerfully handing out packets of colorful advertisements for the show, each extolling the thrills and excitement to be experienced at the performance plus a testimonial to the amazing benefits that could be gained from purchasing a bottle, or several, of Wonder Tonic Cure. As he shoved packets of fliers, sticks of hard candy, and nickel pay-outs into eagerly reaching young hands, he occasionally paused to keep enthusiasm high with a simple magic trick. Then, before sending the band of urchins out to pepper the town with fliers, he paused a final time and, slathering on a generous layer of dramatic flair, gave the assemblage of smudged faces a dire warning. He had "eyes everywhere," he told them, and if any of them tried shirking the duty they had taken payment for by ditching their fliers down an outhouse hole or pitching them into a creek somewhere, he would find out about it and there would be serious consequences.

Tolos, stripped now of his performance costume and clad instead in worn dungarees and scuffed boots for the set-up chores that had to be done before the show could go on, strolled over just as the swarm of boys went tearing away.

"Did you ever think," he said to Wizarious, "that little spiel you always give might do more to put larcenous ideas *into* the heads of those little brats than if you said nothing at all?"

The professor smiled. "Ah, ye of little faith, Mighty Hercules. Don't you realize those little brats, as you call them, are the future leaders of our country?"

"Uh-huh. And the current leaders of our country—corrupt and conniving thugs straight down the line—are what little brats grow up to be. That's exactly my point."

Wizarious chuckled heartily as he reached out and clapped the strongman on the shoulder. "And a valid one it may very well be. But, speaking of connivances, for right now we had best worry about setting up this one of ours in the hope my pack of hirelings scatter enough of those announcements to attract a decent-sized crowd tonight."

* * *

The crowd that night was large and enthusiastic and the performances went off without a hitch. Professor Wizarious mesmerized and amazed with his magic; the Hercules of the High Plains impressed and awed with his feats of strength and displays of muscularity; Beatrice Blaze thrilled with her array of trick shots and marksmanship and then, to close the show, traded her guns for a guitar with which she accompanied herself in a selection of songs ranging from a popular foot-stomper to a lilting ballad and finally a stirring gospel number.

People came away smiling and satisfied and along with them went many bottles of Wonder Tonic—which, it was liberally mentioned throughout the show, played a significant role not only in the general overall health of the troupe but also added extra sharpness to their just-displayed performance skills and talents. If taken as instructed on the bottle, purchasers could expect the wondrous elixir to enhance their lives as well.

No one enjoyed the show more than the man called Smitty, who watched it all from the sidelines. In spite of seeing rehearsal segments out on the trail, this was the first time he'd actually had a chance to view the complete presentation straight through. Although he'd been with the troupe for the better part of a week, at first he was unconscious—in a coma, the professor called it. In that condition (he'd been told, having no recollection of his own) he was present for a prior show in a Wyoming town called Maysfield before crossing over into Nebraska and arriving at Corryton. And, even though he didn't yet have *all* his wits about him, his condition now was improved enough to thoroughly appreciate the performance.

Despite being only a temporary, off-stage part of the troupe, Smitty felt proud and happy for the approving crowd response this evening. He genuinely liked all of the troupe members and was glad to see them reap reward for their hard work. They'd gone out of their way to be kind and generous to him, even giving him some money shortly after they'd hit town today and insisting he buy himself a new shirt and pair of trousers to wear in place of the oversized ones Tolos had loaned him in the interim.

One of the things Smitty figured out about himself was that he had at least a mild case of vanity. So it certainly was a relief to have pants that fit rather than needing to knot a length of rope in two places on the waistband of Tolos' pair and then looping the rope over one shoulder to keep the borrowed britches from falling down around his ankles. He was grateful for Tolos' willingness to literally give him one of the shirts off his back, but at the same time the debt was partly paid by providing the big Greek fodder for plenty of good-natured ribbing about Smitty not having what it took to fill out a "real man's" clothes.

One of the many curiosities about the way Smitty had been found half-dead and half-buried in that rockslide, was the fact whoever did it left him his boots. It seemed a safe bet that they hadn't meant to leave him his life, though, and the fact he hadn't finished dying there at that cave mouth was another debt he owed the Wizarius party.

One more thing he was grateful to them for was that, after bringing him with them and nursing him along the way, they refrained from pressuring him with a lot of questions. Not that he could have told them any more than he did, anyway, but for some reason he had the feeling there were things about himself that, even if he could recall them, he might want to keep guarded. Yet he remained determined to soon find out—to *remember*—what was inside those blank spots continuing to elude him. When he did, he would then decide how much more to share.

But, no matter what else, he knew his indebtedness to these people was going to last for a long time.

* * *

After the costumes had been removed and put away for next time and alternate attire donned, Wizarious gathered everyone at the rear of the changing tent and offered a customary toast—with wine, not Wonder Tonic Cure—for a job well done. Smitty was included, in spite of his reluctance.

And then, in recognition of the evening's particularly good receipts, the professor suggested they all retire to one of the town's dining establishments and enjoy a late supper together, his treat. This time Smitty's reservations were even stronger. He wasn't really part of the show, he pointed out, and therefore had nothing to do with its success and so hadn't earned the right to be included in a celebratory supper. Besides, somebody should stay behind to keep an eye on the camp. He would do that. Secure the horses for the night, start packing up some of the equipment in preparation for tomorrow's departure, and so forth.

"Nonsense," Wizarious said firmly. "In the first place, I have requested and gotten assurance from the town marshal that he will have one of his deputies closely patrol our camp while we step away for a bite to eat. In the second place, you certainly *are* a part of our troupe. You may not have a performing role, but almost from the moment you regained consciousness you've done chores and been helpful in numerous ways around our camps. You pitched right in to help set up the show as soon as we got here today and now you're already talking about getting a jump on tearing down and packing up for when we take leave. Don't tell me you haven't earned the right to come join us."

"But you've already done so much for me," Smitty argued. "What few chores I'm able to help with are the least—"

"All this arguin' is keepin' *me* from a fancy supper," Tolos growled. "If the professor says you should come along, you should come along. Don't make me pick you up and carry you over my shoulder."

Smitty felt himself instantly bridle at the threat, even though he knew it was made in jest. This told him something more about himself—that he had a quick temper he'd have to be careful with.

Before he had a chance to ponder that much further, Beatrice said, "Please, Smitty. We're all famished and my uncle is right—you've clearly become part of our group and you certainly belong dining with us."

The heat that Tolos' remark had caused to crawl up

Smitty's neck now faded just as quickly under the words and gaze from Beatrice. Although she'd always treated him cordially enough, up until that moment he couldn't help sensing a measure of reserve on her part where he was concerned. In fact, this marked the first time he could remember her calling him by name—albeit a made-up one—or initiating any exchange of words between them. Let alone extending encouragement.

"All right. I guess I'm plenty hungry, too," Smitty allowed. He felt his face flush again, this time not in anger. "Only each of you is cleaned up from changing out of your costumes and all. If we're going into the town, can I have a minute to wash up and at least slick back my hair a little?"

Wizarious chuckled at this surprising display of vanity. "By all means. Go ahead."

"Won't do you any good," Tolos called after him as Smitty made for a corner of the tent where a wash basin and mirror had been set up. "If you're looking to strike a spark with any good-looking gals we might run into, kid, they'll never take a second look at you with me around. Beautiful women just naturally flock to me like moths to a flame. They can't help themselves."

–4–

As soon as Smitty was ready, he and the others quit the tent and turned to start across the meadow toward town. It was about a hundred yards from the edge of the meadow to where the town's streetlights started, leaving the distance in between weakly illuminated by the soft glow of the lanterns left burning in the tent along with the cast from above by the ascending moon and a dusting of faint stars. They'd gone only a few steps before they saw a group of half a dozen men approaching through the murky darkness of this empty area.

"Well lookee, lookee here," crowed a short, wiry, bow-legged figure marching a few steps ahead of the rest of the pack, thus giving the impression he was its leader. "If it ain't the wizard hisself, and all his medicine hustlers peeled out of their fancy duds. Tell me, Wiz, does the magic and all that special talent go away when the silk and the grease paint comes off, or is that wonder potion of yours supposed to keep the good juices pumpin' inside a body, no matter what?"

Wizarious came to a halt, as did those walking with him. The wiry man and his bunch strode up to within five feet before they stopped as well, remaining in a loose pack behind the speaker.

"I think," said Wizarious in a totally calm voice, "that I shall refuse to answer such an offensive question posed in such an offensive manner. If you have a legitimate complaint about my tonic, you may come round tomorrow morning before we depart—and after you've had the chance to sober up, I might add—then we can discuss the matter civilly. Should your complaint prove warranted, I will give you a refund."

"Refund?" said the wiry man. "Do I look lame-brained enough to have bought any of that strained horse piss to begin with? I ain't here for no damned refund!"

"What *is* your intended business, then?" the professor wanted to know. "State it and be quick. We've had a long day and we're bound for a well-earned, relaxing supper. We won't be detained by foolishness."

Looking on, Smitty continue to marvel at Wizarious' coolness. At the same time, he sensed the overriding crackle of tension crowding the air—tension, some ingrained instinct told him, that carried with it the very real threat of cold, sharp-edged danger. He didn't know how he was able to discern this so clearly, but that didn't do anything to dull his certainty. He felt his fingertips tingle and small nerves fluttered under the ropey muscles that ran up and down his long arms. He felt the hovering danger, knew he had encountered some version of it before—and knew he was ready to face it again.

The wiry man's mouth spread in a sneer. "Well, ain't that just fine. No problem about it, though. A minute of your time is all it'll take for what I want."

"And that is?"

"I want," the wiry man said, raising his left arm and pointing toward Beatrice, "to shoot against your trick shot artist there." As he said this, his right hand dropped to hover clawlike above the six-gun riding low in a tie-down holster.

Beatrice took a step back as abruptly as if she'd been shoved. "That is ridiculous," she breathed.

"It damn well is!" Tolos exploded. "That's a lady you're pointing your dirty, unwashed finger at, you piece of prairie trash. Put your arm down before I tear it off at the shoulder!"

The wiry man lowered his arm but his sneer stayed in place. "Nobody was talkin' to you, muscle man. You know what's good for you, you'll just stand back and stay out of this."

The rest of the pack shifted up closer behind their man and one of them, a narrow-faced hombre with a scraggly goatee, said, "If the ox has the guts to try anything besides just flap his gums, Jocko, we'll take care of him. Don't you worry about it. You just stay focused on what you came here to prove."

Smitty stood by, lean body poised, silently continuing to watch and listen. Absently, his left hand moved up to his throat, fingers extending as if to touch something that wasn't there. After a moment the hand dropped again.

Tolos motioned eagerly to the men backing Jocko. "Come ahead, boys, let's see how you're going to 'take care of me.' If you think what you saw me do up on stage was all just an act, I'll be happy to give you a personal demonstration what I'm capable of."

"Stop it," the professor said sharply. "There will be no violence here tonight. And there absolutely will be no *shooting* between anyone!"

Jocko's gun, a gleaming Smith & Wesson Double-Action .38—which Smitty recognized without understanding how or why—was suddenly in his hand. His eyes flashed in the murky illumination. "Seems to me," he said tightly, "that me and this smoke wagon have got something to say about whether or not there's any shootin' gonna be done. And we say there is!"

Smitty abruptly realized that his own right hand had drifted involuntarily down and was hanging at his side, fingers curled clawlike in much the same manner as Jocko's had been. There was no holstered gun there for him to grab but—once again with that strange and sudden certainty—he knew that up until very recently there had been. He found himself wishing it was still there.

"My niece is unarmed," Wizarious responded to Jocko. "Same for all of us. Are you prepared to gun down unarmed people?"

Jocko wagged his head. "You don't listen too good, do you? Nobody said anything about 'gunnin' down' anybody. What I said was that I wanted to shoot *against* your pistol queen there. Anybody can plunk targets when they got a bunch of fancy equipment and all the time in the world to take aim. What I'm talkin' about is findin' out who can draw and hit their target *the fastest* … Drawin' too slow sure as hell don't cut it, same as drawin' like lighting and not being able to hit what you're aimin' at. The combination of the two is what counts out here in face-down country, and I aim to show that I'm the fastest and most accurate sumbitch around."

"Sorry, mister, but the show is over," Beatrice said icily. "And I don't do private performances for cow town gunnies who are out looking to show off for a bunch of drunken friends."

Jocko glared at her. "You don't listen any better than your uncle, do you?" He brandished his pistol once again. "*We* are the ones who say when the show is over, not some sassy-mouthed tart. And if you don't watch out, I may have to teach you the kind of private performance you *should* be givin' with that mouth of yours."

"That tears it!" bellowed Tolos, raising his massive fists and charging forward, shouldering Wizarious aside so forcefully he nearly knocked him down.

But two of Jocko's comrades were ready for him. One of them, a fair-sized specimen in his own right, raised his fists, too, and stepped in front of Jocko, bracing himself. Tolos didn't care who was in his in path of intended destruction. He launched a whooshing roundhouse left—what would have been a crushing blow—toward the taunting face of the man who seemed to be begging for it. At the last second, the man ducked and dodged to one side, allowing Jocko the chance to also get out of the way.

The momentum of Tolos' missed punch pulled him off balance and caused him to stagger a half step before he could put on the brakes. That's when the second rowdy backing Jocko's play—the one with the scraggly goatee who'd spoken up earlier—made his move. He threw himself into a low, flat dive, well under the giant Greek's flailing arms, and slammed his full body weight into the side of Tolos' left kneecap.

The sound of ligaments and bones giving way was like the dull pop of a single handclap. Tolos' face drained of all color and took on an agonized expression. He managed to bite off an outcry of what must have been intense pain but he couldn't keep his knees—the just-destroyed one as well as the good one—from buckling. He toppled to the ground.

Wizarious and Beatrice, and even a couple of men from Jocko's pack, emitted sharp gasps at the effect of the vicious attack.

But Smitty, rather than waste time on impotent reaction, saw an opening to take advantage of. Springing with catlike grace and speed, he closed the distance between himself and Jocko as the latter spun away from Tolos' diverted attack. Jocko's movement turned him directly into the path of Smitty. Smitty's hands shot out in a blinding flash, the left clamping on the wrist of Jocko's gun hand. He jerked it toward him and down, simultaneously twisting hard. Jocko made a loud sucking sound through his teeth. His fingers spasmed open involuntarily and Smitty's right hand darted to grab the loosened gun.

Releasing Jocko's wrist, Smitty gave him a disdainful shove and sent him staggering backward into his stunned companions who were struggling to comprehend what had just happened.

Smitty took his own step backward and covered the

pack of troublemakers with a steady left-to-right sweep of the confiscated Smith & Wesson. Over where Tolos had fallen, the bigger of the two men who'd taken him down—not yet realizing the turn of events involving Jocko—was poised with one foot raised to stomp down on the prone giant. Smitty snap-fired without hesitation and the heel of the raised boot was blown away along with an egg-sized chunk of the man's foot. Howling in pain, the would-be stomper pitched into a twisting back flip and crashed to the ground on one shoulder and the side of his face.

The goateed man who'd wrecked Tolos' knee and had then been standing by watching with an eager expression while his partner got ready to do further damage, now reacted by making a belated grab for the gun on his hip. He didn't have a prayer. Smitty's gun spoke again and the slug hit square between goatee and wishbone. The victim, his own weapon never lifting more than an inch out of its holster, did an awkward little sideways hop and then tipped over and hit the ground flat and limp and dead.

While the body was still settling into a heap, Smitty swung back to face Jocko and brought the S&W to bear squarely on his brisket. "Now, you little piss-ant excuse for a wannabe gunslinger, *I'm* the one with the smoke wagon in my hand. So that makes me the one calling the shots. Ain't that the way it goes?"

Smitty had long since taken note that the rest of the rowdies were also packing guns. But none of them seemed in a hurry to try and reach for iron.

Jocko licked his lips, not saying anything. His gaze

was locked on Smitty, eyes filled half with hate, half with fear.

"I asked you a question," Smitty snarled through clenched teeth. "A minute ago you had all kinds of mouth slop to shovel. Now you've suddenly dried up?"

"Take it easy, Smitty," Wizarious spoke up in a soothing voice. "You've done a good job of taking control of a bad situation, don't let it go back out of control now."

"Don't worry about me," Smitty told him. "You want to worry about something, go over and check on Tolos. Beatrice, probably be a good idea for you gather up the guns from those fallen men."

Beatrice and her uncle, mouths set tight and firm, moved silently to do as suggested.

"What about my men?" Jocko said to Smitty. "I didn't hear you tell anybody to check on them."

"The one's past checking on, the other I don't give a damn about."

"That's mighty cold, mister."

"You're the one brought it all on, no use to cry about it now."

Smitty gestured to the others standing behind Jocko. "The rest of you men drop your gun belts and step back," he said. Then, to Jocko, he added, "But not you. You stay put."

One of Jocko's eyes twitched. "You ain't gonna just gun me where I stand, are you?"

"Somebody ought to," Smitty said.

Jocko swallowed. "Man, that's a helluva thing to say."

"Tell that to the goateed gent over there you got killed."

Up in the town, things were starting to stir. People who'd heard the shots were venturing out into the street to see what was going on.

A lone figure with a drawn gun and a lawman's star gleaming on his chest was double-timing it toward the meadow.

Smitty considered for a long moment. His left hand once more drifted up to his throat as if seeking something there, then fell away empty. His eyes flicked again to the approaching lawman. When they cut back to Jocko, some of the heat had gone out of them. "You're a lucky man," Smitty said, in a voice so low it was almost a whisper.

–5–

"I can't help thinkin' we're pushing our luck, that's all," Clem Driscoll was saying. A worried frown tugged at his expression, making his whole face droop in concert with his sagging walrus mustache. "We got the biggest stash we ever put together at one time before in our lives. Hell, maybe as much as double. And only four ways to split it. We could make the divvy right now and each be able to lay off easy for a good long spell."

"That might be one way to look at it," Everett replied, allowing his older brother to have his say yet unable to keep traces of annoyance and impatience out of his voice. "But with our new method working so smooth, why not stick with it a ways farther? Ride it for all it's worth. We can put together an even bigger stash, then lay off easy for an even longer spell."

"Stick with it how far, Ev? When is it going to be enough?"

"I don't know. I don't have a specific dollar figure in mind, if that's what you mean." The strain in Everett's tone indicated his patience was wearing thinner. "But, dammit, I know we can do better than only settlin' for what we got. It'd be like sittin' in on a poker game with a tableful of suckers and all of a sudden just walkin' away, leavin' winnings behind you know you could rake off easy as pie. Why would anybody do something like that?"

The two men stood at the edge of a sparse cottonwood grove, gazing out across an expanse of empty high plains terrain. Dark, fast-moving clouds skidded across the nighttime sky, letting through only brief spurts of starlight and rare glimpses of a pale moon.

In one hand, Everett held a tin cup containing the cold remains of some whiskey-laced coffee that he'd carried with him when he strolled out from camp to speak privately with his brother. Clem, Winchester balanced against one hip, was in position to take the night's first watch. At the campsite in the middle of the cottonwoods, Vint Brenner and Burt Ketchel had already turned in.

Moving on from the rhetorical question he'd left hanging in the air, Everett spoke again, in a lower voice. "How long we been doin' this, Clem?"

"Bank-robbin' and such, you mean?"

"Uh-huh."

"Well … 'bout a dozen years, I reckon."

"Closer to fifteen." Everett raised the tin cup to his mouth and took a sip. Lowering it again he continued. "Sometimes I can't hardly remember anything that came before. 'Cept the war, of course. All I know is that once we started down this road … well, we been goin' down it ever since."

"It's a long one," Clem allowed. "Ain't no turn-offs after you've gone too far on it. Like we have. It only ends at a prison gate or on a gallows."

"Or with a bullet," Everett added. "We've seen a lot of good men reach the end that way, too. Blood kin, a good share of 'em."

"Too true."

"I think that's the part that bothers me the most. Losin' those brave lads—a lot of 'em blood, like has been said, and some of 'em so damn young to boot. They shouldered up next to us, looked to us to lead 'em safely in out of the scrapes, lead 'em clear of the bullets and the posse hounds. Too often we fell short on that."

"They were young, but old enough to know the risks when they signed on. Same as the ones we took."

"I know. I used to get by on tellin' myself that same thing. But hell, back at the beginning, when I was a lot younger myself, there was a wild spirit in me that actually *liked* bein' in the thick of the chases and the flyin' bullets. I figured anybody would just naturally be excited over the same opportunity."

"Yeah, you were plenty wild," said Clem, smiling a bit wistfully. "Guess I sorta was, too, even though I was a little older."

Everett drained the tin cup and sighed. "Reckon I must be gettin' mellow in my old age, though. Ain't sayin' I necessarily regret all the things we done. But, lookin' back now, I can admit where we could have done some of them different. Most likely smarter and better, in the long run."

"But it's all water under the bridge now, little brother."

"Yeah. Water under the bridge. Blood in the ground."

Clem regarded his sibling. “You’re in a mighty peculiar mood tonight.”

“Reflective, I guess you’d call it. Like I said, I must be gettin’ mellow in my old age.”

“Uh-huh. Mellow … but you still want to ride out and hit more banks just as quick as we can.”

“Yeah, I do. And you don’t get it, do you? You don’t understand at all what I’ve been trying to explain.”

Now Clem showed signs of being the one starting to get annoyed. “What explanation? We’ve been talking about our wild young beginnings and the fellas who rode with us and ended up biting the dust. You saying there was supposed to be some kind of connection between that and this new bank-robbin’ streak you’re so hell bent on continuing? If that’s the case, then no, I don’t see what one has to do with the other.”

Everett sighed again, this time deeper and louder than before. “Those fellas who bit the dust after choosin’ to ride with us—you know how many there were in fifteen years, big brother?”

“No. Can’t say as I kept count.”

“Thirteen. How’s that for a nice round, unlucky number? Thirteen in fifteen years. Nine kinfolk, four others who joined in for one reason or other. Plus a half dozen or so others we sent packin’ because they got too shot up and crippled to do us any good anymore.”

“You’ve kept right tidy track, haven’t you?”

“Didn’t always. But I been rollin’ it around in my head quite a bit lately. I think I got it tallied pretty damn accurate.”

"Okay, Ev," Clem said, his tone suddenly sounding weary. "I can see all that is important to you. I respect that. But I'm blamed if I understand what it has to do with our current situation."

"Look. We just hit three banks in less than two weeks. Like you pointed out a minute ago, we've got a bigger stash put together right now than we ever had before at one time. *And* we did it without adding a wisp of gun smoke to the air. Except only once, in Yuba City, thanks to that stupid, greedy bank manager and the town's spineless sheriff."

"They forced your hand. You didn't have any choice," Clem said.

Everett frowned. "Not with the bank manager. But it probably wasn't necessary to include the sheriff, too. I lost my damn temper. You know how much I hate gutless bastards, especially ones who try to hide behind a badge."

"No harm done, though—except to those two who asked for it. We still made it out of town with no serious trouble."

"Exactly." Everett's frown fell away and his expression took on a kind of eagerness. "That's my whole point about how slick this new method is working and why I want to stick with it. We ride into these towns nice and easy, we ride out nice and easy. And in between we fool the local law and the bank big shots into cooperating so eagerly they damn near get down on their knees and offer to polish 'The Marshal's' boots."

Clem chuckled. "Yeah. They really hop to it for that

badge, don't they?"

"Like I told you, in my wild younger days I might've got a kick out of the chases and the blazin' guns. But I've had enough of that. Easy in, easy out suits me fine. And I don't have to worry about seein' any more of our boys shot out of the saddle ridin' next to me. Or wounded so bad we end up havin' to bury 'em out in the wild somewhere."

"Amen to that. With only four of us left, we can't afford to lose nobody more."

"That's why I want so bad to stick with this deal we got cooking. We target three or four more banks, ride hard between the towns, strike quick and smooth before word spreads too far and wide about our imposter marshal set-up."

"There's the part I'm worried about. It's going on two weeks since Yuba City. Not to mention the other two. Don't you figure word has already spread pretty damn wide by now?"

"All the more reason for us to move fast," Everett insisted. "And we don't go after the big towns and big banks, where they're apt to get the word first and expect us to most likely to hit. We go after the smaller places, not aimin' for one *big* haul but puttin' together a string of lesser ones, like we've done so far. You figure we already got double the most we ever had? What if we double that again? Hell, we might wind up with enough to break away entirely from this dirty business and strike out in a whole new direction."

Clem's eyes brightened. "You mean that, Ev?"

"I said it, didn't I?"

Clem regarded his brother closely. “It’s just that, well, I never heard you say anything like that before.”

“Christ, Clem,” Everett said, grinning crookedly. “You think my intent has been to keep livin’ on the dodge, like this, forever?”

Now Clem grinned, a little sheepishly. “I was hopin’ the hell not. But, like I said, you never indicated anything different.”

“Well I’m indicatin’ it now. Okay? We keep after this thing the way I want to, put together a poke as big as I figure we can, then California is just a-beckoning. It’s warm all the time there, but not so warm it fries your damn skin—just comfortable warm. They got hot-blooded women by the wagonloads out there, each one friendlier and more beautiful than the next. And they claim the mountains and hills are so full of gold they practically piss it out in the streams. You don’t even have to dig for it. But that won’t matter to us, ’cause we’ll already have out pockets lined before we ever get there!”

Clem’s smile stretched wide. “That sounds like the place for me!”

“For *us*, big brother,” Everett corrected him. “We’ve come this far together, that’s how it stays.”

Clem’s smile faded. “But ain’t we gonna take time for a visit back home before we go?”

Eyes narrowing, Everett said in a raspy voice, “What for? Nothin’ left there for us any more. Ain’t been for a long time.”

—6—

Following the incident in the meadow, the Wizarious show troupe was detained in Corryton for an extra day. The town marshal was a cautious, methodical man. Having had previous trouble with Jocko and his rowdy pals, he harbored little doubt they'd been the main cause. But a man had been killed. That, combined with the anonymity and faulty memory of the shooter—a man known only as Smitty—was what moved the marshal to take extra time and investigate the situation more closely than he otherwise might have.

In the end, though, he was sufficiently convinced that the actions of Smitty were justifiable self-defense and so he and his companions were given the nod to depart. The release was accompanied by a none-too-subtle hint suggesting that, in order to avoid future confrontation in case of lingering hard feelings, the extravaganza probably ought to scratch Corryton from its performance circuit the next time or two it passed through the area.

The local doctor who tended Tolos' damaged knee also took an added interest in the matter of Smitty's amnesia. He had no first-hand experience with the condition, but he'd read a number of documented cases and seemed to find the subject fascinating. When all was said and done, however, he turned out to have far more questions than answers. All he could offer as a final analysis—based as much on hunch as professional conclusion—was the opinion that Smitty's memory would restore itself completely in due time.

When the wagons rolled out of Corryton early on the second morning, there was no cheering throng to see them off the way there had been to greet their arrival. Only the taciturn, expressionless town marshal was present, watching them leave from the front porch of his jail building.

* * *

Standard procedure had always been for Wizarious and Beatrice to travel in the front wagon, whose box carried the costumes, show paraphernalia including pieces of backdrop scenery, food supplies, cooking utensils, spare clothes, and various other odds and ends. It also contained a pile of bedding for occasions of inclement weather when Beatrice would spend a night in the wagon. The men, fair weather or foul, settled for bedrolls underneath the wagons.

The second wagon, with Tolos as the sole teamster, until Smitty came along, was packed tight with the show tents, staging equipment, spare wagon parts and tools, and cases of Wonder Tonic.

Now, however, Tolos' injury—which made it necessary to keep his leg straight and thus negated any reasonable way for him to sit a wagon seat, especially while bouncing over rough country—called for different arrangements. After much protesting and cursing, the strongman was forced to accept the fate of riding in the box of the first wagon (because there wasn't enough room in the second), propped up on Beatrice's blankets with his leg cushioned and thrust out straight and stationary.

When it had come time for the wagons to roll, Smitty, expecting to have the second rig to himself, was more than a little surprised when Beatrice strode back and climbed up on the seat beside him.

"With Uncle grousing and lamenting about losing a day's travel and Tolos carrying on about being treated like an invalid," she explained airily, "it was an easy decision to separate myself from their misery. This way I can have some peace and quiet and they can grumble and curse the air blue, if they like, without worrying about trying to control their language for my sake—which they never succeed in doing, anyway, when they're in foul moods like this." She turned her face abruptly and gazed full at Smitty. "You don't mind if I ride with you, do you?"

The answer was easy. "Not at all." He was keenly aware of her nearness and her beauty but, where only a day or so earlier it would have made him feel uncertain and ill at ease, it now only brought the enjoyment of being in the company of an attractive woman.

Since the incident in the meadow—or, more specifically, the part he'd played in it—Smitty had been feeling more confident about most things. He still had blanks that needed filling in, to be sure; but now, instead of having anxiety over what they might turn out to be, he had an eagerness to know, a more positive sense of what would be revealed.

The morning started under a muddy gray sky. Before long, however, the gray began to disperse and then expanding patches of blue and eventually the sun itself broke through. Watching, Smitty couldn't help thinking that the change was not unlike the way his memory was gradually emerging from whatever was clouding it.

As the morning brightened and warmed, conversation between Smitty and Beatrice flowed more and more freely. In one way it seemed rather curious, considering how they'd mostly skirted around one another and how little they had spoken before this, yet at the same time it felt quite natural and relaxed.

As they approached the Nebraska-Wyoming border, Beatrice told Smitty about Lusk, the little Wyoming town where they were headed to play their next show. She said, "It's a nice place and, even though it's small, we usually draw a good crowd there. It's part of the regular circuit we've established over the past three or four years. Corryton was, too. But that mule-headed marshal made it plain enough we're not going to be welcome back there, at least not for a while."

"Thanks to me, I reckon," muttered Smitty.

Beatrice's eyes flashed. "Nonsense. Don't you dare try to assume any of the blame for what happened. There are thanks due you, that's for sure. But *not* in a negative way. If it hadn't been for you, who knows how badly we would have suffered at the hands of those roughnecks the other night? Especially after they took Tolos down—it was obvious by what they were getting ready to do to him what kind of savagery they were capable of."

"Yeah, we can't forget that. The real thanks should go to Tolos," Smitty pointed out. "If he hadn't charged into them the way he did, bare-handed, I would have never gotten the opening to do anything at all."

"Both of you were incredibly brave," Beatrice allowed. "But there were too many guns against us if you hadn't managed to get hold of one yourself."

"Like I said, I'd've never got the chance without Tolos."

"What's more," Beatrice continued, "once you had the gun you pretty convincingly demonstrated a skill with it. Any idea where that came from?"

Smitty cut her a sidelong glance as one corner of his mouth lifted briefly in a half-smile. "I thought when I got clear of the marshal and the doctor back there, I'd also be clear of questions for a while."

"I'm sorry if I'm prying, but … well, there's still so much unknown about you. I realize that probably no one wants the answers to your past more than you do yourself."

"You'd be right about that."

"Recognizing as much, I think my uncle and Tolos and I have been very restrained about pressuring you."

"Yes, you have. And I'm grateful."

"But after the other night, the way you handled that gun … I thought perhaps it might've jogged something in your memory."

"Something I wasn't willing to reveal to the marshal or the doctor, you mean?"

Beatrice looked taken aback. “I didn’t mean for it to sound that way.”

“Don’t worry about it. If I *had* flashed on some big, new revelation, you’re probably right—I wouldn’t have let on to a couple of pushy strangers like them. At least not until I had a chance to think it over and share it first with the folks who took me in and showed so much patience with me.”

“That’s very gallant. But from your words, I gather you *didn’t* recall anything new?”

“Afraid not. Well, except for one thing.”

“And that is?”

“I remembered that … yeah, I can see it even more clearly now … the reason I’m pretty good with a gun, see, is because I used to be a sharpshooter with a traveling medicine show!”

It took a moment for Beatrice to realize Smitty was having a little fun at her expense. Her expression went from mildly stunned to uncertain to comprehension followed by a flash of mock anger. “Oh, you smug jester you! That wasn’t funny at all!” She swatted his shoulder with the back of her hand. But a moment later she couldn’t suppress a bubbling laugh.

“I’m sorry. I couldn’t resist,” Smitty chuckled.

Beatrice tried to scowl at him but couldn’t hold it. “You really had me going, didn’t you?”

“Judging by the look on your face, I guess I did. I hope you’re not sore. Really, I don’t make a habit of joking around like that.”

“Don’t be silly. I can take a joke as well as anyone.” Beatrice smiled, as if to prove the point. Then, aiming to sink a little revenge barb, she added, "But what I want to know is, with that fractured memory of yours, how do you know how big a joker you may or may not be?"

Smitty's expression turned thoughtful. "I'm not sure. I guess, growing up with the Arapahos, I never saw much that seemed funny enough to—"

He stopped mid sentence. His thoughtful expression deepened, his gaze shifting abruptly to something far away. He took all of the reins in his right fist and his emptied left hand lifted absently to touch a spot at the base of his throat.

"You do that often, touch your neck like that," Beatrice observed. "Did you have an injury there? An old wound or something?"

Smitty shook his head faintly. "No. No wound."

Beatrice regarded him even more closely. "And what did you mean when you said 'growing up with the Arapahos' a moment ago?"

Smitty continued to gaze at something far away. "I'm not sure. But I think I'm starting to remember."

–7–

"An Arapaho tribe," Smitty was relating in a flat voice, almost a monotone, "took me in after my white parents were massacred. I was just an infant. My Arapaho mother was named Elina. She called me White Deer. She nurtured and loved me as her own, and I responded in kind. My father was Lightning Cloud, the chief of the tribe. He was devoted to my mother, so he put up with me mainly in deference to her. He taught me how to track and hunt, how to fish, how to survive in the wilderness. He taught me the ways of a warrior and set me on the path toward becoming a man."

The troupe was gathered around a small cooking fire, having halted for their nooning in a shallow bow-like depression, thick with greening grass across its bottom and a narrow, twisty creek running through the middle. A hot wind was gusting across the high plains landscape that surrounded them, but down in the bowl and in the notch of the V-pattern formed by how they'd parked their wagons, they were out of most of it. In the sky overhead, the clouds that had broken up earlier had now begun to reform and gradually darken once more, as they were wind-whipped from one horizon to the other.

"When I was twelve, my mother grew ill and passed

away," Smitty went on. "At the same time, my tribe was preparing to relocate north, into Canada, to get away from the growing flood of white men pouring across our lands. I made the choice not to go with them. My father agreed. He said the time was right for me to return to the race of my birth and seek my future with them."

"Mighty harsh, turning a lad of twelve out into the world to seek his own way," muttered Wizarious.

Smitty shook his head. "It was my choice, too, remember. And while Lightning Cloud was a hard, stern man who never warmed to me, he nevertheless took the time and showed the patience to teach me everything he knew, everything he thought was important for a young man to survive on his own. Still, with Elina no longer there to calm the waters between us, like she always had, we both recognized my place was no longer with him or the Arapaho."

Beatrice sat silently, watching and listening. She had already heard all of this earlier, in the wagon, as the recollections initially burst free from one of those blank pools inside Smitty's head. The retelling now was for the sake of Wizarious and Tolos, and also for Smitty to scour that formerly blank pool in order to make sure he reclaimed everything that was there.

"It's good that you were able to remember all that stuff, kid," said Tolos, from where he sat on a wooden crate of Wonder Tonic Cure with his injured leg extended and propped on a pillow resting atop another crate of the same. "But what about the rest of it, the part that came after you left the Arapaho? Not to short-change ol' Lightning Bolt, but—"

"Lightning Cloud," Smitty corrected him.

"Right. Him. The thing is, it for sure wasn't him who taught you how to handle a gun the way you do. Right?"

"No, it wasn't," Smitty confirmed. "Lightning Cloud taught me strictly the traditional Indian ways. Guns didn't play a part."

Seeing the direction the conversation was headed and sensing that Smitty might be uncomfortable with it, Beatrice spoke up. "What came next, after Smitty split from the Arapaho, is where his past turns fuzzy once again. But the important thing to keep in mind is the significant progress he *did* make in recalling as much as he has."

"That's for sure," Wizarious agreed. "It's not only significant for how much he remembered, it proves that his memory overall is healthy and churning hard and it's just a matter of time before everything else returns."

"Let's hope the rest of it is something really good," Smitty said, managing a grin. "Maybe I'll turn out to be a wealthy businessman or landowner. Heck, maybe even a duke or earl from somewhere."

"That'd be rich—a gunslinging earl," said Tolos. "The Earl of Six-Gun Manor. That's got a nice ring to it, wouldn't you say?"

"I'd say you're being rather insensitive, if you want to know the truth," Beatrice said sharply. "I hardly think Smitty appreciates having his condition ridiculed."

"It's all right," Smitty told her. "All meant in fun. I'm the one who started it, actually. It's okay."

"That's right," said Tolos. "If I'd've really wanted

to ridicule something, I would have gone after his other name … the dainty and delicate 'White Deer.' What kind of name is that for a hell-raking, scalp-taking, widow-making Arapaho warrior riding out on the war path?"

Tolos was still talking when Smitty's attention was drawn by movement up on the eastern rim of the grassy depression. A moment later, three wind-buffeted riders appeared up there, reining their horses to a halt and then peering intently down at the campsite, their blurred expressions unreadable.

"It's clear that your injured leg hasn't done anything to slow your tongue," Smitty said tight on the heels of Tolos' rhetorical question. "But how about the rest of your musclebound carcass? If the need came, how quick could you roll off that crate and find cover under the nearest wagon?"

"Ducking for cover has never been my strong suit," Tolos huffed. "But, if I was of a mind to, I reckon I could manage it okay. What's your point?"

Smitty said, "Don't everybody look at once, but we've got visitors up there on the rim. Can't say exactly why, but my gut feeling is that they don't mean us well."

"That's good enough for me," Tolos responded. "What do you want us to do?"

"Just be ready. For right now they're only giving us a good looking over. When they decide to ride down, I figure it'll play out quick enough."

"In the meantime, if they *do* have bad intentions," said Wizarious, "we're bunched up here like sitting ducks."

"Well then, let's get a little *un*-bunched," Smitty said. "Beatrice, how about you take the coffee pot over to the water barrel on the side of the wagon? Rinse it out good and then refill it, like you're going to make a fresh pot. Take your time."

"All right," said Beatrice.

"That wagon is where your show guns and shell belts are, right?"

"Yes."

"Near side, or far?"

"Far."

"Good. If any trouble breaks out, I want you to scramble under the wagon and get to the back side as quick as you can. Get to where you can make a grab for your guns."

"Got it."

Beatrice picked up the coffee pot and started toward the water barrel with it.

"What about me?" Wizarious wanted to know.

"The wagon I've been driving has a Winchester rifle in the front boot. Yours?"

"It does too."

Smitty nodded. "Good. That's the one closest to you. Same thing, then. Visualize how it's placed in there, get ready to make a grab for it if need be."

"We can't be certain they mean us harm."

"Like I said, we're just bein' ready in case they do."

"And if it comes to that, all you expect from me is to roll for cover and not do anything to help?" Tolos growled.

"If any of us has the chance, we'll get a gun to you," Smitty told him. "But it won't do you much good if you're too riddled with bullets to be able to do anything with it—so, yeah, your first order of business is to haul your ass to cover."

Beatrice had reached the water barrel by then and was beginning to rinse out the coffee pot. Up on the rim, as if at some unseen signal, the three riders gigged their horses and started down the slope toward the camp.

Smitty turned to face them, squaring his shoulders, planting his feet wide. His right arm hung loosely at his side and this time there was a gun ready at the fingertips. It was a single-action Colt Peacemaker, nickel-plated with a pearl handle, riding in a black leather holster trimmed with silver studs. The rig was from Beatrice's arsenal of show guns and had been presented to him after the trouble back at Corryton. Everyone in the troupe felt it might be a good idea for Smitty to go armed following that incident … and now their foresight seemed on the brink of paying off.

The riders reached the bottom of the natural bowl and came across the grassy flat at a gallop. When they drew closer they slowed their animals.

Smitty said, "That's far enough."

The horses stopped and then stood pawing the ground, nickering a bit at the smell of water in the nearby creek.

The center rider, a thick-waisted, middle-aged hombre in need of a shave, with a wad of chaw bulging out his bewhiskered left cheek, said, "I bid good morning to ya'll. Now, don't you find that a mite friendlier way to greet folks when you come across 'em?"

"In the first place," Smitty said easily, "morning fell away about a half hour back. In the second place, I don't recall there bein' anything especially good about it while it was here."

Bulge Cheek leaned forward and rested a forearm across the top of his saddle horn. One half of his mouth curved with a humorless smile. "Are you just naturally a contrary cuss, or is there something about the sight of us that chaps you for some particular reason?"

"State your business," Smitty said. "We can decide the rest of it from there."

The rider to Bulge Cheek's left, an older man with a rodent's face and one gnarled yellow tooth poking down over the lower lip just off center of his mouth, said, "I'd say this jasper has got a downright snotty attitude. He must think gettin' away with the stuff he pulled back in Corryton makes him some kind of special somebody who can say or do whatever he wants."

"You men from Corryton?" Smitty asked.

"Thereabouts," came the answer.

Smitty felt an icy trickle run down his spine. Hearing this bunch was from Corryton, combined with that "stuff he pulled" remark, pretty much confirmed the bad feeling he'd had at first sight of them. Their showing up here wasn't happenstance. They'd followed the troupe, come after them with a purpose—and not likely a charitable one.

"You see," Bulge Cheek went on, "we ride for Anse Ambret's spread, the Double Bar A brand. You might've heard of it. It's one of the biggest around—and it's also the brand those two men you shot the other night rode for."

"Apparently this Ambret fella ain't very choosy about who he hires," Smitty replied.

Bulge Cheek's eyes narrowed. "Since I just identified me and my pards as also ridin' for the Double Bar A, you don't give me much choice but to take that as a flat insult, mister."

"Take it however you like. You can thank your other pard—Jocko—for givin' me what you might call a biased outlook."

"Nobody said that snotnose Jocko rode for our outfit. Ol' man Ambret culled him out a good while back. I said I was talkin' about the two men you shot."

"Then they should have had the sense to cut Jocko out of their circle of pals, too. You want to blame somebody for what happened to them, the blame lies square on his shoulders and their own poor decision to side with him."

"That snotty attitude comes with a right sharp tongue, too," said the snaggle-toothed rider.

The third man, to Bulge Cheek's right, spoke for the first time. He was a tall, blade-faced hombre with intense dark eyes and a twisted mouth that moved only at one corner when he talked. "Whatever his attitude, ain't no denyin' there's something to what the man says. The way Jocko kept proddin' to prove himself as some kind of half-assed pistolero is what got him run off our spread to begin with."

As the blade-faced man said this, Smitty regarded

him more closely. There was something about the speaker—something going on behind the dark eyes—that demanded tighter attention. And the way those eyes were looking back at him, boring in deep, Smitty somehow sensed the man was also seeing something more than the medicine show roustabout he'd come riding after.

"Anse could see Jocko's trigger-happy ways were sooner or later bound to set bullets a-flyin' and possibly get innocents hurt in the bargain," the blade-faced man continued. "Well, that's exactly what *did* happen. And who was behind it more than Jocko?"

"So what?" Bulge Cheek demanded. "The bottom line is that two Double Bar A riders ended up shot. One of 'em shot dead. And it wasn't Jocko's bullets in either one. If Anse was around, instead of bein' off on that trip to Omaha, ain't a doubt in my mind that's how he'd see it. He'd want payback from the one who planted the bullets, not somebody who might've been yappin' on the sidelines."

"That's right," chimed in Snaggletooth. "Why the hell did you ride with us all morning if you wasn't figurin' to settle the score? You think we came here just to talk mean to this sonofabitch for shootin' up our boys?"

Under different circumstances, Smitty would have opened the ball right then and there. The talk of payback and settling the score made it clear beyond any doubt that the intent of these men was to call him to task for his gunning down their two pals … except for the blade-faced man. Whatever his intentions had been in the beginning, something appeared to have changed. And whatever it was, it had to do with with what he saw when his eyes bored into Smitty.

Did the man recognize him?

Almost as confirmation of this, Blade Face responded to his companions, saying, "No matter what we started out to do, what I'm tellin' you now is that goin' up against this man for what happened back in Corryton is a bad idea." He was still gazing at Smitty, studying him, as he spoke. Then, abruptly, he looked away and cut his gaze over to the other two, adding, "You can count me out. I'm heading back."

"Like hell you are!" hissed Bulge Cheek. "Nobody does me that way."

"If you know what's good for you, you'll call it a day and ride away with me."

Smitty realized he didn't want the blade-faced man to ride off. He suddenly had questions he wanted to ask him. But the tension that had been clamping tighter over the scene became too much and Frank Wizarious thought he saw an opening to take action. With a desperate, trapped-animal sound erupting from his throat, the professor wheeled about and lunged for the driver's boot of the front wagon, making a grab for the Winchester positioned there.

With his back to the wagons, Smitty couldn't see this, he could only hear the curious sound Wizarious made. But there was no mistaking Snaggletooth's reaction. The old 'puncher went rigid in his saddle and began clawing for the six-gun riding on his hip.

Smitty's reflexes were instant and lightning fast.

The perfectly balanced Peacemaker—which he'd had the chance to practice with at considerable length back in that Corryton meadow—leaped into his fist almost as if by its own volition, gliding smooth as a whisper from the silver-studded holster. It twice barked flame and smoke before Snaggletooth's hand even closed around the grip of his own pistol. Both slugs slammed tight together into the man's chest, scarcely an inch from his heart, and he was knocked into a backward somersault off the rump of his horse.

The bottom of the bowl broke into a frenzy of wild activity. Shots exploded, horses reared up, mules screamed, blue gunsmoke billowed.

Wizarious seized the Winchester he'd reached for and spun back around with it, jacking a shell into the chamber. Two bullets from the gun of Bulge Cheek slammed into the side of the wagon just below the professor's left elbow. He snapped off a return shot but it went wild over Bulge Cheek's head as the horses still hitched to the wagon lurched in their harnesses and caused the wagon to jerk forward, knocking Wizarious off balance.

Immediately after downing Snaggletooth, Smitty pitched himself into a diving roll meant to dodge any return fire. He came up on one knee with the Colt raised and ready. Bulge Cheek, after getting his shots off at Wizarious and seeing him stagger, was now twisting in his saddle and bringing his arm around to draw a bead on Smitty. But Smitty was quicker on the trigger. He felt the Peacemaker buck again in his fist and saw a thumb-sized red dot appear in the middle of Bulge

Cheek's forehead. The Double Bar A rider's hat went flying from his head, lifted by a geyser of blood and brain matter, as he toppled to one side and spilled to the ground.

Wizarious, regaining his balance after nearly being knocked down by the wagon jolt, got off another shot at Bulge Cheek but it came as he was already starting to fall after being struck by Smitty's round.

Tolos had scrambled to safety under the same wagon the professor was shooting from. His booming voice could be heard bellowing for somebody to throw him a gun.

Beatrice, as instructed, had also made a dive under the wagon containing her guns and, although momentarily out of sight, was presumably now in back scrambling to get her hands on one of the weapons.

The remaining horseman, the blade-faced man, poured lead in the direction of Wizarious, forcing him to duck low, pinning him down and preventing him from firing back with the Winchester. From where he was crouched, Smitty couldn't get a clear shot at Blade Face due to the jerking and rearing of the riderless horses previously sat by Bulge Cheek and Snaggletooth.

A part of Smitty still wanted a chance to ask the blade-faced man about the recognition he thought he saw flare in those dark eyes. But now, with lead flying, there seemed damn little chance of that—not without risking somebody from the wrong side taking a bullet.

At that instant, Bulge Cheek's mount jerked back out of the way and, through the roiling dust, Smitty had a clear view of Blade Face. The latter sensed this in the same moment. Like Bulge Cheek only a minute before, he twisted in his saddle and started to swing his aim toward Smitty. Whatever had caused his earlier reluctance to get involved in a shootout no longer mattered. Everything had broken loose, and it was now a fight for survival.

Smitty didn't hesitate either. He fired, shading his aim slightly, trying for a shoulder hit. He succeeded, seeing the right shoulder—the base of the shooting arm—blossom brilliant red. Blade Face's torso jerked and his gun flew from his hand.

Smitty surged to his feet and began running forward, Colt still raised and extended at arm's length.

Blade Face teetered in his saddle, reaching with his left hand to clasp the blasted shoulder. At that point, a rapid burst of three shots rang out, all striking Blade Face square in the chest.

Startled, Smitty stopped running. His face snapped in the direction of the wagons. Beatrice was emerging from between them in a haze of gun smoke, two gleaming pistols held quick-draw fashion at waist height.

Blade Face toppled to the ground.

Smitty turned back and ran the rest of the way to where he'd fallen. He dropped to his knees and lifted the man by his shoulders. The head rolled loosely but those dark eyes still held a faint flicker of stubborn life.

Smitty shoved his face close. "Who am I? Do you know me?" he shouted.

The eyes fluttered.

"Do you know who I am?" Smitty demanded.

A bubbly exhalation escaped out of the riddled chest. And then, from the twisted mouth, came a ragged sound that might have been a word. "Lara … mee."

After that, nothing.

–8–

"Hooo-wee! Look at 'er come down," Vint Brenner marveled as he gazed out a lopsided window of the crumbling sod shack.

The night outside raged with a late spring thunderstorm. Pitchforks of lightning criss-crossed the sky, each time followed by a rumbling protest of thunder, as if the sizzling bolts were inflicting wounds in the boiling black clouds. Wind-whipped sheets of rain slapped relentlessly against the outside of the soddy.

"Man. This storm's almost as fierce as the one that damned ol' Marshal Laramie almost trapped us in the other night."

"Both mighty fierce, that's for sure," agreed Burt Ketchel from over by the crackling fireplace, where he was pouring himself a cup of coffee. "Hard to believe," he added, "that other one was only a couple weeks ago."

"Yeah, a powerful lot's happened in between." Vint turned his head abruptly and looked back at his comrade. "I wasn't thinkin', Burt. Sorry if me bringin' up that other storm stirred memories about the loss of your brother."

"Don't worry about it. He's already in my thoughts a lot, anyway."

"Yeah, I suppose he is. I miss Bob, too. Always liked havin' him around."

Burt blew across the top of his coffee cup, eyes following the swirls of steam as they spun away and dispersed. "Everybody liked havin' Bob around. He was that kind of fella."

Vint returned to gazing out at the storm. Wanting to change the subject away from Bob, he said, "This keeps up, come morning we might need a damn boat to make it out of here."

"Just be thankful we found this place," Burt replied after taking a drink of his coffee, "or we'd be out there smack in the middle of it. A bug-infested old wreck of a soddy might not be much under normal circumstances, but tonight it seems like a doggone palace."

The sod hut, along with a collapsed wooden lean-to barn and corral attached to its back side, had once served as a switching station for a freight line running between Cheyenne and Deadwood. The existence and name of the line had long since faded from memory. But there was enough left of its structures, dilapidated though they may be, to still offer a welcome slice of shelter on this otherwise stark expanse of open land.

Just as Burt was stating his appreciation for the same, Everett and Clem Driscoll came in from where they'd been confabbing out in what was left of the lean-to barn. Each carried a bulging canvas bag. Since the roof of the lean-to was less intact than that of the soddy, rivulets of rainwater were skimming off their hat brims.

Nevertheless, Everett was wearing a broad grin.

"Did I hear right? What talk is this of a palace, Burt?" he asked.

"You're standing in it," Burt answered, making a gesture to indicate their surroundings. "Leastways, that's how it seems on a night like this." He shrugged. "Or that's the point I was trying to make, anyway."

"And it's a damn good one," Everett agreed. "Like they say, everything is, whatycall, relative."

Vint frowned. "What is that supposed to mean?"

"Means to a starvin' man, a crummy, half-moldy old biscuit can seem like a feast. Means to a freezing man, the raggediest old blanket you can imagine is like a fine quilt bedcover. And so on."

Vint shook his head. "I've heard that kind of talk before. But I never could quite get the grasp of it. A moldy biscuit is always gonna be a moldy biscuit, far as I can see. Same for a ratty old tore-up blanket. How can either one be any more or any different than what they are?"

"Nobody's sayin' they can actually *be* more," Clem Driscoll joined in somewhat exasperatedly, trying to help get the idea across. "But circumstances can sometimes make 'em *seem* like a lot more."

Everett waved his hand. "Never mind. The kid just ain't been through enough hard times to understand. Praise the blessings on him for it." He paused, letting his mouth spread into another grin, this one with a sly twist to it. "What's more, the way things are lookin', the lucky son sure as hell ain't gonna be facin' hard times in the foreseeable future, neither."

"Ain't sure I follow you," said Vint.

By way of an answer, Everett hoisted the bag he had carried in from the lean-to and plopped it onto the rickety remains of an old table. “You know what this is, don’t you?”

Vint nodded. “Sure. It’s part of the stash that’s piled up from this string of bank jobs we been pullin’.”

“You bet it is. How much you figure is in here, total, this bag and the other one Clem’s holding?”

“Don’t rightly know. We been ridin’ so hard and hittin’ banks so fast I never took time to try and figure. Can’t say I haven’t thought about it, though, and I reckon it’s got to be a mighty tidy sum.”

Clem chuckled. “Mighty tidy, indeed.”

Burt straightened up from beside the fireplace and stepped over to stand with the others around the table and the bags of money.

“By the count me and Clem just took out there in the lean-to,” Everett said, “we got close to a quarter of a million dollars in these bags. To say it another way, that’s near two hundred and fifty thousand dollars, gents.”

Vint’s eyes grew large and bright. Burt gave a low whistle.

“That’s five banks in only a little over two weeks,” Everett went on. “A lot of hard ridin’ and quick-hittin’, like the kid said.”

“And thanks to this sham of using Cash Laramie’s identity and his marshal’s badge and all,” Clem pointed out, “we’ve done it with only four men and only one time ever havin’ shots fired.”

“In case you don’t realize it,” Everett added, “that’s

an impressive accomplishment. Maybe even a damn record of some kind."

Vint was still staring wide-eyed at the canvas bag. "I ain't past tryin' to get my head around a quarter of a million dollars yet. I never dreamed I'd see that much money piled in one place at one time."

"Well, it ain't finished growin' yet," said Everett. "It's gonna increase by whatever amount we haul out of one more bank. Then we're done. The ruse we've been using with the marshal's badge and all is a beauty, but we can't keep it up forever. We've made it work by ridin' hard and sweeping far, always hittin' small towns and small banks where word hasn't yet spread about the bluff we're running. We get dumb and try to push it, though, one of these times we'll ride into even the smallest burg and they'll be laying for us."

Burt nodded. "Be nice to take our divvies, get off the hard ol' trail, and just lay low in comfort somewhere for a nice long spell."

"Not gonna be that way. Not this time," Everett corrected him. "Oh, we're gonna make ourselves nice and comfortable, no doubt about that. But it's gonna be for more than just a spell—it's gonna be forever! After we hit that bank in Lusk, the town east of here where we're headed, the Driscoll gang will have rid its last ride on the outlaw trail. We'll divvy up our haul, say our farewells, then go our separate ways."

"Forever?" Burt echoed. He looked suddenly crestfallen, almost panicky.

"You're bustin' up the gang? For good?" Vint sounded as if such a thing was another concept he couldn't quite grasp.

"You heard right," Clem confirmed.

"Look at you two," Everett scoffed. "You'd think I just announced we were gonna cook and eat your favorite horse or something. Christ Almighty, it's every outlaw's dream to someday make a big enough score so's he can afford to quit the wild ways and finally settle down somewhere. Leastways, it's supposed to be. What's with you lunkheads—you tellin' me you was *lookin' forward* to nothing but robbin' and ridin' all your born days?"

"It's all I've ever known … since the war," Burt pointed out.

"Same for me," said Vint. Then he quickly added, "Not the war part, I don't mean—I was too young for that. But I was just seventeen when my pa got killed and you took me in to start ridin' with you. You fellas are the only family I got."

"Yeah, and why is that?" Everett demanded rather harshly. "Because too many of our kin, leastways on the menfolk side, got killed either in the war or turnin' against what passed for The Law afterward. The Driscolls, Ketchels, Brenners, even a good share of Todds and Mullers—core kinfolk and shirttail relatives, too—all got swept up in it, seemed like.

"We left pain and poverty and despair to go fight a winless war, then came home to even less than was there to start. Only now we'd learned how to fight back against stacked odds, not just knuckle under to 'em. So we took the guns ol' Abe and General Useless Grant was benevolent enough to leave us and that's what we did. We fought back some more. They called us 'outlaws' for it. So that's what we became."

Everett paused abruptly. He let his head hang, as if he'd either run out of words or just grown weary. His thick-fingered hands gripped the canvas bag tight, knuckles turning white. Then he lifted his face and his eyes burned into Vint and Burt as he spoke again.

"But bein' outlaws was *never* meant to be the end of the line, boys," he said. "We saw it as our only way out, our only way to fight for a chance at something better. And now we four are lucky enough to have made it. We owe it to the others who didn't—your pa, Vint, and your brother, Burt, and all the rest—to make it count for something."

"You two are a sight younger than me and Clem. Especially you, Vint. Practically your whole lives ahead of you. If you don't take this chance and make something good out of it—a family, kids, a solid place in some community where your past never has to catch up with you—then you'll be bigger disappointments and bigger damn fools than I ever took you for."

Everett paused again, this time only briefly. A wistful smile played across his weathered face. "Me and Clem, not bein' so young, probably ain't got the family thing in store for us. Not a family of our own, I mean. But that don't mean we ain't still got our dreams. We'll be chasin' 'em out Californy-way as soon as we're done here."

"But do we have to split up?" Burt said plaintively. "Can't we come to California with you? Can't we chase our future out there, too?"

"If we're gonna bust up the gang, it'd be best to bust it up all the way," Clem said, his expression stern. "No matter how clean we try to go after this last job, we got things hangin' over our heads that are gonna keep some folks on the hunt for us for a long time to come. We stay in any kind of bunch, it'll only increase the risk of drawin' attention, maybe causin' somebody to take a second look that might lead to suspicion or, worse still, recognition." He shook his head. "Just because we quit outlawin' don't mean we can ever let our guard down for havin' lived that life."

"I reckon I can see how it has to be that way," Burt allowed reluctantly.

"Look," said Everett, taking his canvas bag off the table and setting it on the floor next to Clem's, "we still got time to put the finishing touches on our plans after the last job is done. In the meantime, we got us a nice dry place to weather the storm that's rippin' outside so I say let's take advantage of that much and enjoy our good fortune one piece at a time. I smell coffee cooking, but I don't smell no grub. I'm hungry as a wolf, how about the rest of you?"

There was quick consensus that everyone else felt the same.

"I was gonna set some bacon to fryin' once the coffee was brewed," Burt admitted with a sheepish grin as he started back over to the fireplace. "But I guess I got sidetracked by all the talk of how rich we are."

After leaning over to dig a frying pan and a side of bacon out of their supplies pack, Burt straightened up and turned part way to face the others again. "Seems to me, though," he said, "that a fella who's due a cut of over a quarter million dollars ought to have a maid or butler or some such to do his cooking and serving for him."

"That sounds reasonable," Everett agreed. Then, fighting to keep a straight face as his gaze traveled meaningfully up and down Burt with his frying pan and slab of bacon, he added, "And it looks to me like at least three of us *do*."

There was a pause, long enough for a low growl of thunder to roll in from outside, and then everybody—including Burt—broke into a round of hearty laughter.

* * *

Two miles southwest of the abandoned freight station, a lone rider was also encamped for the night. His accommodations were far less hospitable.

With a folding shovel taken from his possibles pack, he'd scooped a horizontal dugout into the northern bank of a steep-walled gully, just under the rim and well above the gurgling rush of rainwater now filling the bottom of what for most of the year remained a dry wash. He'd positioned himself in this manner so that the slicing rain and wind coming out of the north blew over and away from his dugout, rather than slanting in on him.

Above, just over the rim, the man's grulla horse was picketed securely. The animal was a hearty breed, toughened even more by many hard miles and years in the wild country. It seemed outwardly oblivious to the storm and stood munching the sweet, rain-freshened spring grass within the picketed area almost nonchalantly.

Tucked into the dugout along with saddle and saddlebags, the man stretched out warm and dry. Like the grulla, he also had been toughened by life experiences both prior to and currently as part of his job wearing the badge of a deputy U.S. marshal.

Minus the luxury of a cooking fire, he'd eaten a cold supper of jerky and hardtack. And now, wrapped in a bedroll covered over with a waterproof slicker, he puffed contentedly on his pipe and considered his lot to be not all that bad. He knew that the men he was pursuing were only a short ways ahead of him and he had a pretty good idea where they were headed. The satisfaction of this knowledge and the confidence that he would soon be catching up with them went a long way toward overcoming any temporary discomfort he had to endure.

Still, as revealed by a flash of lightning that showed the man's dark countenance gripped by a somber expression, there was a deeper concern eating at him. Catching up and dealing with the Driscoll gang was one thing; a task he felt capable of being able to handle and was even looking forward to.

But if there was any truth to reports the marshal had recently received—reports he refused to believe, yet could not ignore altogether—then catching up with the Driscolls would also mean catching up with the facts behind those reports. And, depending which way those facts swung, he might end up facing something he didn't know if he was truly prepared for or not.

–9–

After the shootout with the Double Bar A riders, the medicine show troupe traveled another dozen miles, crossing on into Wyoming, before setting up night camp ahead of the massive storm front rolling in on them out of the northwest.

They turned the wagons against a low outcropping of ragged rocks that thrust spine-like out of the ground, close enough to gain some wind blockage but not so close as to take on rain runoff from the higher ridges. The horses were fed, watered, and hobbled securely. The troupe members scarcely had time for a cooking fire and a hasty meal before the rain hit.

After that, there was nothing left but for each of them to try and find a dry spot to hole up and wait out the storm and the night. Despite his protests not to be coddled, Tolos' injured leg rated him the bed up in the wagon box. Beatrice and Wizarious took slicker-wrapped bedrolls under the lead wagon; likewise for Smitty under the rear wagon.

At first, it was just the rain. Pouring down hard and cold. Then, gradually, the wind and thunder moved in and the storm intensified.

Smitty was glad for the chance to be alone. He let the storm envelop him like a giant cocoon, isolating him from everything but his thoughts. He needed the time to rehash recent events in his mind. To explore different possible interpretations, to once again go deep inside himself in order to try and root out more answers from the remaining blanks.

There had been almost no talk amongst the troupe following the mid-day shootout. They'd merely made sure each other was okay, then reloaded and put away their guns, broke camp, climbed up on their wagons and departed, leaving behind the faint stink of cordite hanging in the air and three dead men sprawled on the ground.

Without explanation, Beatrice had elected not to ride with Smitty and instead, once again, chose the lead wagon seated next to her uncle.

Smitty had naturally wondered about that, but at the same time he appreciated the chance for the alone time to ponder the situation leading up to and culminating in the recent shootout. Now, under the wagon in the rain, he wondered again about Beatrice's choice. But, more than anything, he kept thinking about the look he'd gotten from that blade-faced Double Bar A rider—the expression he'd taken to be recognition. Is that what it really had been? And what of the frustratingly nebulous final word the man had uttered?

"Lara ... mee."

What the hell was that supposed to mean?

Smitty was aware of the town of Laramie located west of Cheyenne. And, closer still to their present location, down to the south, there was the old fur trading post and later Army camp called Fort Laramie. Did he have some association to one or both of those places?

Or had the utterance perhaps not been a broken single word, but rather two separate words? "Lara" could be a woman's name. But what of "mee" then? If it was meant to be the rest of a name, maybe Blade Face hadn't been able to get it all out. Maybe *it* was a broken word. But what? *Meeker … Meachum ... Meeney ...*

Smitty tossed in his bedroll and cursed under his breath. The storm continued to roar and rumble. He squeezed his eyes shut and willed himself to calm down. If he didn't hold his frustration and anger in check, he knew, he wouldn't get anywhere.

Calm down, damn it.

Let the storm blot out everything else.

Think …

* * *

Smitty woke with a start. Surprisingly, what with the howling storm and all that was on his mind, he somehow had managed to fall asleep.

It wasn't the shriek of the wind or a crash of ground-trembling thunder that stirred him, however. It was the awareness of someone slipping hurriedly, somewhat frantically into his bedroll with him … a body cool and naked, slick from the rain, and possessing the unmistakable curves and softness of a woman.

"Wrap me in your arms," Beatrice's voice demanded in an urgent whisper. "Hold me tight, warm me … make love to me!"

Smitty complied without hesitation. He folded her in his arms and pulled her hard against him. His hands glided over the hills and hollows of her sleek, splendid body. Her flesh warmed and grew feverish under his touch. They kissed hungrily.

"Are you sure this is what you want?" he husked as their bodies entwined.

"I've never been more sure of anything in my life," she replied breathlessly.

They coupled then, their lovemaking as fierce as the raging storm. Once they had climaxed, they lay back exhausted, bodies slick and beaded with sweat, nearly as drenched as if they were exposed to the downpour that continued to fall from the boiling sky.

With her head cradled on Smitty's arm, her breathing finally beginning to level off along with his, Beatrice murmured, "That was everything I hoped for, everything I knew it would be."

"For me it was more than that, because I never dared hope for such a moment," Smitty told her.

"It's not exactly something I make a habit of doing," Beatrice assured him. "But after the events of the past few days and hours, filled with so much menace and killing … I guess I needed reassurance that something tender and sweet still existed in this harsh old world."

Smitty grinned in the darkness between lightning flashes. "Sweet, yes. But tender? I don't know about that. Gal, you make love like a wildcat."

Beatrice slapped him lightly on the stomach. "Don't be crude."

"If you say so."

She left her hand resting on his taught belly. "That man I shot today … for all the bullets 'Beatrice Blaze' has fired in her illustrious career, that was the very first time I ever pulled the trigger in earnest, aiming to hit another living thing and not just a paper target."

"I'm sorry you had to do that."

"I saw him drop his gun and realized you had hit him," she went on. "But when he reached across with his other hand the way he did, I thought he was going for a second gun, a hideaway under his coat or something."

"So you shot to save me. For that I'm grateful," Smitty said.

"Only there *wasn't* a hideaway gun, was there? And your shot was intentionally meant to wound, not kill. You wanted him alive so you could get some answers out of him, the way you tried even after I shot him. Did you recognize that man, did you know him from your past?"

"No. More like the other way around. From the way he acted, I had a hunch he recognized me. I was hoping for the chance to find out if that was really the case."

"But I ruined it by killing him."

"When bullets start flying, you have to act fast and decide faster. Nobody's faulting you for what you did. Hell, it was probably just my imagination anyway. That hombre most likely acted the way he did because, when it came right down to it, he started growing a yellow streak at the thought of facing up and trading lead."

"Are you just saying that to make me feel better?"

"Maybe," Smitty allowed. "But all that really counts is knowing your intentions were good. Anything else would be fretting over what we can't be sure of and couldn't change even if we was."

They lay quiet for a minute or two, listening to the sounds of the relentless storm. As they'd talked, Beatrice's hand had drifted idly up from Smitty's stomach and come to rest in the center of his chest.

Lightly, Smitty placed his hand over hers. After a moment, he said, "It was an arrowhead talisman, a gift from my Arapaho mother just before she passed away."

"What was?" Beatrice asked.

"Earlier today, you wondered why I'm always reaching up to touch here at the base of my throat. It's a habit I hadn't even been aware of. But now, having recalled my early years with the Arapaho, I remember the gift of the talisman and how I wore it on a leather thong so that it always hung there."

"So, even through the fog of your amnesia, you kept reaching for it. For comfort, for reassurance," Beatrice said.

"I guess."

"Your love for your mother obviously is very strong, strong enough to reach places where even your conscious mind could not."

"My love for her is very strong, yes, but so is the pain of having lost her. Who's to say which was the one strong enough to reach through?"

Beatrice was silent for a moment before replying, "It doesn't really matter, I don't think. What matters is that, as long as she is alive in your heart and memory, she isn't really completely gone."

"Perhaps. I wish I could be as sure as you sound."

"It's the age-old question," Beatrice told him. "Is it

better to have loved and lost, or never to have loved at all?"

When Smitty had no response for that, Beatrice said with a sigh, "And there's the rub—no one ever has the definitive answer."

Once more they lay still and quiet in each other's arms, as if momentarily isolated from the storm and all else.

Then, softly, Beatrice said, "Not to pretend that what we're doing here tonight falls under the category of deep, devoted love or anything … but there nevertheless is affection and caring involved. I sense that, very soon now, you will be leaving us. Before you go, I want you to know that, despite the circumstances and brief period our time together will have been, you'll remain fondly in my memory for a long time."

"I appreciate hearing that. Same goes for me toward you. But I reckon we both knew from the start I'd be riding on eventually."

"I suppose. But it didn't matter so much before."

"Nothing in the future—not tomorrow, not the next minute—is a sure thing, gal. All you can do is live in the moment and live it to the fullest."

"Is that what we're doing now?" Beatrice said.

Smitty reached for her and pulled her hard against him once more. "Wouldn't you like to think so," he said huskily.

* * *

Smitty woke again with a start, this time to a brilliant, white-hot blast of lightning and a shattering explosion of thunder that marked the peak of the storm. The fact he was alone, that Beatrice had departed at some point earlier, was no part of his conscious thoughts. His only concern, that which sent him immediately into frenzy of shoving and scrambling, was to get untangled from his bedroll. To his mind it had transformed into something more than just a bedroll. It was a pressing, grinding weight somehow unleashed by the storm. He was being squashed and smothered by it. When he tried to open his eyes, he couldn't see—not even the dazzling streaks of lightning. And when he opened his mouth to cry out, it immediately filled with something bitter and gritty that stifled any escaping sound and turned into a desperate scream that began echoing shrilly inside his head—

So violently did Smitty kick free of the nightmare and his bedroll that he pitched out from under the wagon and tumbled full into the open, exposing himself completely to the onslaught of the wailing storm. Rain gushed down on him. A thousand electric fingers of lightning clawed the sky. Thunder shook the ground and sent vibrations through his body where he lay sprawled upon it.

The power of the storm not only rattled the earth, it also rattled his memory.

With growing excitement, he recalled another violent storm.

Not so very long ago.

His eyes were shut tight against the pouring rain but his mind's view, filtered through a sudden rush of recollections, was plain as day.

The storm ... The sentry he'd had to kill ... The narrow-mouthed cave ... The Driscoll gang inside ... His patient vigil in that narrow opening ... The rockslide collapsing down on him with terrible suddenness ...

Just like that, it all came into focus. Everything. With crystal clarity.

What had happened. Who he was!

"Lara … mee," he murmured.

Then, continuing to lay flat on his back, facing straight up at the furious sky, he said in a louder voice, "Cash Laramie."

His mouth spread into a wide, rake-hell grin. His voice grew louder still. "I'm Cash Laramie, you hear that, you puny-ass excuse for a storm?"

Now he began laughing and his voice rose to a shout. "You think you know how to bring the thunder, Mr. Storm? You don't know shit! I'm Cash Laramie, and nobody brings the thunder like I do. You watch, I'll show you how it's done. I'm back—all the way back—and I got a job to finish. You happen to see those Driscoll boys who left me for dead, you tell 'em, you hear me? You tell 'em they're real soon about to get some thunder visited on them like nothing they ever saw before."

He continued to lay there, naked, laughing and shouting at the storm, until Beatrice and Wizarious finally emerged from under the lead wagon and coaxed him back to shelter.

–10–

Frank Wizarious gave another incredulous wag of his head. "I just can't get over it," he said for the third or fourth time. "Traveling our show circuit over the past twenty-odd months, we've heard the name Cash Laramie—the most renowned U.S. marshal in the territory—so many times. And now this. Having you right here in our midst, without a clue, this whole while."

"And for much of that time," Beatrice said ruefully, "I held fast to a suspicion you were some kind of desperado."

"Sometimes, out in the wild corners of the frontier," Cash replied, "you can run into situations that cut a fine line between the law and the lawless. If you heard my name mentioned often enough, you likely heard me referred to as 'the outlaw marshal' a time or two."

Wizarious gave a measured nod. "Yeah, I guess that did come up on a few occasions. But most of the time, by far, when Cash Laramie is spoken of it tends to be in quite favorable terms."

In the first light of a new day, the show troupe was gathered around a cooking fire, reviewing the revelations that had come to Cash so dramatically the night before—the final pieces of the puzzle that had been locking out the memory of his complete identity.

Each member held a tin cup of strong coffee poured from the pot resting on the coals of the fire. Also on the coals sat a large skillet containing thick strips of bacon just beginning to sizzle.

The full orb of the sun had risen above the eastern horizon only minutes ago, casting a pinkish gold glow into the now cloudless sky. The storm had passed on in the dark hours. The taller prairie grasses remained somewhat flattened and slick-looking from the deluge. A few small puddles, sparkling as the early sunlight skimmed over them, stood in the creases and dents across the top of the spiny rock outcropping behind the wagons.

By noon, all these signs would be erased by the heat of the new day, and last night's storm would only be a memory for those who'd endured it.

"Even without knowing his name or reputation, you'll remember it didn't take long for me to peg our boy Smitty as an okay fellow who'd only just fallen on some hard luck," Tolos reminded everybody from where he was once again seated with his injured leg propped on a case of Miracle Medicine Cure.

Offering a reminder of her own, Beatrice said, "We know his name now. You can stop calling him Smitty."

"I know, I know." Tolos held up a hand defensively. "You gotta give me a while to get used to that."

Cash smiled tolerantly. "You can call me whatever you like, big man. As I've said before, I'm deeply obliged to all of you for the way you took me in, gave me the benefit of doubt, and nursed me to my senses again. If not for that, I'd've stayed half-buried in that rockslide and ended up exactly the way the Driscoll gang thought they'd left me—dead."

"With your quick actions over the past few days," Wizarious pointed out, "you've more than squared any indebtedness you might feel you owe us. The question now is, what's your next move?"

"Yes," Beatrice said. Her eyes were probing, apprehensive. "Where will you go from here?"

Cash took a sip of coffee, finding it hard to meet Beatrice's gaze. "First stop is Lusk, just like our plan has been all along," he said. "Just because I've finally got some things straight in my head, doesn't mean I'm going to bail out quick as a snap and leave everybody in a lurch. Especially not with Tolos injured and all. I'll stick around long enough to help get set up and put on tonight's show. Exactly what comes next can be decided after that."

A chuckle rumbled deep in Tolos' massive chest. "Spoken like a real trouper," he said.

"Once we hit town," Cash continued, "I'll naturally want to swing by the telegraph office and get a message off to Devon Penn, the chief marshal over in Cheyenne. After not hearing from me for so long, he probably figures me for dead. Hell, it might ruin his day to find out otherwise. At any rate, once we've re-established contact, I'll be asking about any recent activity that can be traced to the Driscoll bunch. Not to sound like I'm bragging but, once they had reason to figure I was off their trail and out of the way for good, I can't hardly believe they've been laying low and behaving themselves like good little boys."

"So as soon as you get a line on them," said Beatrice in a tight voice, "it'll be just a matter of time before you ride out on their trail again … the men who already left you for dead once."

This time Cash had no trouble meeting her gaze. He held it with a firm, flat one of his own. "It's what I do, Miss Beatrice. A little detail like them leaving me for dead only makes it all the more important for me to get back after them."

* * *

The lone rider approached the abandoned freight station cautiously. The day was building bright and clear, a faint breeze stirring the air. With the sun climbing toward its noon peak, the grass cover over the thirsty, sand-based soil had already lost all but a faint trace of dampness, the final remnant of the previous night's rain.

From a low, distant hill, Gideon Miles had been watching the soddy when four men rode away thirty minutes earlier. The magnifying lens of his spyglass had aided in identifying each one of them, confirming what he'd already known in his gut. The Driscoll gang—brothers Everett and Clem, cousin Burt Ketchel, nephew Vint Brenner. The best part of this visual reaffirmation, however, wasn't so much the faces he *did* see, but rather the lack of a new one alleged to have joined the others, according to claims recently passed on to Miles. While that determination was something of a relief, he nevertheless still found it disconcerting to note that one of the horses being ridden away bore a striking resemblance to another steed he had more than a passing familiarity with.

Ground sign from the recently departed riders was easy to spot. It was all around the soddy and the tenuously attached wooden lean-to, and matched perfectly with what he'd observed from the distance. The men were headed east and slightly north.

"Lusk," Miles said to his grulla mount. "Not much doubt about it, especially since there's nothing else out that way."

When the grulla offered no argument, Miles added. "That gives 'em plenty of time, so they weren't in a hurry to head out and won't be in no hurry along the way. Seein's how we'll need to circle wide around 'em, though, in order to reach the town and make arrangements ahead of time, you'll need to hoof it a mite smarter, Smoke."

Once again the grulla had no comment, argumentative or otherwise. At the faintest nudge from Miles, it simply started off in the direction guided and at the prescribed pace.

* * *

"I don't know about the rest of you hard-eyed hombres," Vint Brenner was saying as he and his comrades plodded along at an easy pace, "but I'm feelin' kinda sad, knowin' we're headed for our final job together. It's like … I don't know, sorta like you're gettin' ready to call it quits with a gal who's maybe a little rough around the edges but has always been faithful and devoted. You got the itch to move on because you figure you can do better somewhere else, but at the same time you feel kinda sorry for what you're ending. Anybody understand what I'm sayin'?"

"I sure as hell don't," said Clem Driscoll, riding next to him. "How is trading a dirty, dangerous life on the run for something safe and stable with a future anything like dumpin' a plain woman you've grown tired of and going on the prowl for something flashier, probably turn out to be a harlot?"

"The kid's, whatycall, a romantic," Everett, riding on the other side of Clem, tried to explain. "He's young and high-spirited, sees things through the eyes of a poet. An idealist. He ain't worn down and practical like me and you, thinkin' back on what could have been the best years of our lives and havin' to look past the tattered edges of all the wanted posters they put out on us to see even a glimpse."

"Hey, that was kind of poetic in its own way," Vint said. "At least Everett gets what I was trying to say."

"What I think *I* get," muttered Clem, "is that poetry and horseshit sound an awful lot alike."

"That's because you're too damn serious. You ain't never had a romantic bone in your body," Everett told him.

"Tell the truth now, Clem," Vint said earnestly. "Don't you have a lost or abandoned love somewhere in your past? Some gal you took a shine to but had to leave behind when you lit out for war or to ride the outlaw trail?"

"I've taken shines to plenty of gals in my life," Clem

admitted. "But once we settled on the price and I'd laid down my money, we loved hell out of one another for as long as I could afford then I went on my way without either one of us left pinin' over it."

Everett shook his head, at the same time unable to hold back a lopsided smile. "See what I mean? You're hopeless."

"What about you, Burt?" Vint asked the remaining member of the gang. "What do you think about all this lost love and new beginnings business?"

"The only thing I got time to think about right now," Burt answered, "is decidin' what to do with my share of a quarter million dollars once we finish this last job and make the divvy."

"What to do with it?" Vint echoed. He wagged his head as if in disbelief. "Man, oh man. I got enough dreams and notions to cover the lot of us. No sir, for damn sure *I* ain't gonna have no trouble findin' high-livin' ways to spend my cut!"

Everett and Clem exchanged glances.

"And what kind of high-livin' plans have you got in mind?" Everett wanted to know.

"Well," Vint drawled, "since you and Clem have staked your claim on Californy and made it clear nobody else is welcome to join you there, that sort of narrowed my options for where I could take my money and start livin' it up. But that didn't slow me down for very long. New Orleans is where I decided. No bitter-ass winters to suffer through, spicy jambalaya to eat and sweet mint juleps to wash it down, a choice between refined southern belles or hot-blooded Creole maidens to pass the leisure hours, and a wide open city where an enterprisin' lad with a wad of cash like me can make the biggest splash since ol' Andy Jackson hit town."

Clem grunted. "Uh-huh. And what about after that wad of cash gets dwindled down? Which'll take about a month, the way you're talkin'. Unless some back bay hardcases chunk you over the head and take it all at once, that is. Then what? You'll be nothing more than a little tadpole in a great big pond and the only splash you make will be a tiny ripple no one even notices."

Vint scowled. "You're always ridin' me, Clem. What the hell? You think I'm that much of a clueless hick I won't get no farther than you're claimin'?"

"New Orleans is a big, bad city. It's chewed up and spit back a hell of a lot tougher hombres than you. That's all I'm sayin'."

But Vint wasn't ready to let it go. "Yeah, well it ain't ever spit back me 'cause it ain't never seen the likes of me. That's what I'm sayin'!"

"Knock it off, the both of you," Everett growled.

"There's some air-clearin' needs to be done," Vint insisted. "Clem has talked down to me and treated me like nothing more than a tag-along ever since I joined this outfit. But I was so bustin' proud to be ridin' with the same bunch my Pa had been part of that I bit my tongue and looked past it and only kept tryin' that much harder to show I was up to the measure."

Everett's warning glare grew hotter but Vint ignored it and continued having his say. "Now, by God, I think it's time for somebody to admit I *am* pulling my share. And more, to tell the whole of it. This stash we've been able to put together, the successful campaign of bloodless, lightning-fast robberies that raked it all in—can anybody deny it was *me* pulling off such a gutsy act as a federal marshal that made the whole works go as smooth as it did?"

Clem hauled back on his reins. "Now wait a goddamn minute. I've heard about a bellyful of that kind of hogwash!"

All four riders came to a halt, horses switching around to form an uneasy semi-circle.

"So have I, kid," Everett said through clenched teeth. If the words and the fire in his eyes weren't enough to make his meaning clear, the way his right hand hovered over his holstered Colt drove the point home beyond any doubt. "The day any member in any gang of mine thinks he's bigger than the whole, then that's the day we need to have a real serious come-to-Jesus talk."

"I never said I was bigger than the whole," Vint replied, pulling in his horns a little but still poised to show he wasn't off the prod completely. "I just want it recognized my part ain't no unimportant, hind-tit-suckin' one, neither."

"Nobody ever said it was. We all know you been doin' a helluva fine job playin' that federal marshal part. You're the center of attention for makin' the whole ruse work. Gotta be a lot of pressure each time, and you held up every time we counted on you. If you'd've stumbled or come across fake to any of those law dogs, the whole thing would've fallen apart."

"I give you your due for that," Clem allowed.

"Never meant to let on otherwise."

"Why do you needle me all the time, then?"

"'Cause you're cocky. You annoy me," Clem answered bluntly. "Our sainted mother used to have a sayin' reminds me of you: 'I'd like to buy him for what he's worth and sell him for what he thinks he's worth,' she'd say. Don't mean you ain't got decent worth, just means others might see it as bein' not quite so high as you do."

Vint contemplated the words for a minute, then said, defensively, "Fella don't think well of hisself, how can he expect anybody else to?"

Now it was Clem's turn to contemplate and the chore pulled his face into a deep frown.

At the same time, it drew a wide grin out of Everett. "Well," he said to Clem, at length, "kid's waitin' for an answer. Tell you the truth, I kinda am too."

"Then how about you two—since you're both poets or romantics or whatever—figure it out for yourselves? Otherwise, if you're waitin' on me, you can keep waitin' till your asses fall off." With that, Clem wheeled his horse around and gigged the animal once again in the direction of Lusk.

With Everett still grinning, the others silently followed suit.

After an hour or so, Everett and Clem lagged behind Burt and Vint to a point where they could talk in low voices without the other two hearing.

His grin now replaced by a thoughtful expression, Everett said, "You're right about the kid. He's too damn cocky. We're gonna have to kill him before we let him wander off on his own."

"Uh-huh," Clem agreed.

"Ain't a matter of greed or angling for a bigger slice of the pie or anything like that. Strictly for the sake of our own survival. We leave him on his own with that cocky attitude and mouth of his, it'd be just a matter of time before he'd go to blowin' and braggin', tryin' to impress somebody, and he'd say something that would sick the bloodhounds on us, even out in Californy."

"Uh-huh," Clem said again.

"I think Burt will be okay."

"We don't have to worry about Burt."

"But we can't take a chance with the kid and his mouth."

Clem nodded. "I'll take care of it. I was figurin' to, anyway."

–11–

Approaching from the east, the Wizarious show troupe came within sight of the town of Lusk shortly past noon. With their destination now close at hand, this left them the opportunity to stop for a mid-day meal. After that, the wagons would be hung with bright strips of bunting, the performers would don their own colorful costumes, and the timing of their actual arrival would be geared so that they rolled down the main street at a prime point in the afternoon, sure to draw as much attention as possible.

Prior to leaving a town where they had just completed a performance, Wizarious made a habit—providing the necessary services were available—to wire ahead to their next scheduled stop and arrange for the newspaper there to place an ad announcing the big show was on its way. He'd done this before reaching Corryton and had done so again, notifying Lusk, once the marshal's interrogation cleared them to depart.

While the delay in leaving had initially frustrated the professor, it didn't take him long to figure out a way to advantageously use the extra time.

First, he and Tolos worked out a revised routine that would allow the strongman to still put on a performance in spite of his injured leg. This meant eliminating anything where necessary for Tolos to have to stand up. Instead, they came up with alternative feats of strength he could accomplish while seated on a sturdy base constructed of lumber nailed around a heavy cottonwood stump. These included bending iron bars; twisting horseshoes; arm wrestling challenges to the brawniest men from the audience; tugs of war where teams of three, lined up on either side of Tolos, would tug on a rope to try and pull his arms apart once he had his hands clasped—or, alternately, try to prevent him from drawing his extended arms inward and folding them across his chest while teams were again pulling in resistance.

Once these new wrinkles were designed and ready to implement, they comprised a display of raw power nearly as impressive as the previous routine.

What's more, to "sell" the notion of Tolos' damaged leg and to give it its own added impact, Wizarious concocted an imaginatively modified version of how the injury occurred. With permission from Cash to minimize the role he truly had played in the Corryton meadow incident, the professor created an embellishment that told of Tolos beating back the six thugs with his bare hands until his knee was nearly destroyed by sheer weight of odds and a vicious blind side attack—at which point, Beatrice Blaze was forced to resort to her lightning-fast pistols in order to finally and fatally conclude the violence encounter.

To give this tale full credibility, Wizarious conspired with the Corryton newspaper editor (a notorious tippler who turned out to be bribable by a palmful of coins and a free case of Wizarious Wounder Tonic) to print an exclusive copy of the *Corryton Courier* featuring—in place of the actual article that appeared in every other edition as distributed to the general public—the professor's embellishment, in bold type splashed across the front page, of how things had gone that night in the meadow. It was Wizarious' intention to use this doctored news account at the start of the Lusk show—and probably for several others thereafter, if it worked as well as he calculated—to help "pump up" the crowd. He would present and then pass around the newspaper as irrefutable proof of what extraordinary individuals—thanks in no small part to regular doses of Wonder Tonic, he would be sure to mention—his two star attractions truly were.

Watching and listening to all of this, Cash once again marveled at the professor's quick mind and intuition for showmanship. To a degree, he even admired it. Thinking now as a marshal, it crossed Cash's mind that if Wizarious ever turned his cunning to a life of crime—real crime, that was, not the basically harmless flim-flammery that was part of his current trade—he would make a very challenging adversary.

Further ruminations along these lines were interrupted by Beatrice moving up beside where Cash stood sipping coffee as he watched Wizarious and Tolos doing some fine-tuning to the revisions they'd made for the strongman act.

"For someone who isn't going to be part of our 'extravaganza' for hardly any longer," she said quietly, "you certainly continue taking a keen interest in the proceedings."

"In case you never noticed," Cash responded, "your uncle is a fascinating man."

"Yes. Life with him has never been boring."

Cash wasn't sure what to say to that so he drank some more of his coffee and said nothing.

"You're doing it again," Beatrice said.

"Doing what?"

"Touching where you used to wear your arrowhead."

"Must have been a habit I formed while I was wearing it. Likely going to be a hard one to break."

"Do you suppose it was taken by the men who left you for dead?"

Cash shrugged. "Either that, or it got torn off in the rockslide. Not much doubt they took my guns and my horse. Maybe my badge, maybe it got tore off in the 'slide, too. Makes sense for them to take the guns and the horse. The badge, possibly to ridicule or brag about. But the talisman, I don't see why they'd have any interest in that at all. Maybe I'll get the answer when I catch up with the Driscolls."

"If any of them are still alive."

"There's always that."

"Or if you're alive to do the asking."

"There's that, too." Cash's eyes gazed off at something Beatrice could not see. "But I'd put a helluva lot higher odds on one over the other."

* * *

They rolled into Lusk with all the standard hoopla. The

wash of dazzling afternoon sun heightened the bright colors of the bunting draped over the wagons and winked off the spangles on Beatrice's costume and the oversized belt buckle of the belt strapped around Tolos' waist. Professor Wizarious' spiel rolled out enticingly and the bunches of people who came to line the street responded with eager eyes and voices, applauding and cheering at the teasing snippets of entertainment meant to draw them to the full show later on.

Cash, who normally didn't care all that much for noisy crowds, drove the second wagon with stone-faced attention to duty but at the same time couldn't help but feel pleased with the exuberance of the reception.

Once again after receiving a go-ahead nod from the town marshal, Wizarious steered the troupe to the far side of a small grove located a ways down from a good-sized livery stable. It was here they would set up for the evening's performance.

By prearrangement, as soon as the wagons were parked in place, Cash quit the others and headed back into town on foot. His purpose there was twofold: First, due to Tolos' limited mobility and the remaining matter that would keep Cash himself occupied for an indeterminate length of time, he needed to find two able-bodied men who'd be willing to hire on for the task of helping to set up the show tents and performance stage under the direction of the professor. Next, he needed to pay a visit to the local telegraph office—which he'd spotted on the way in—where he would begin trading wires with Devon Penn in Cheyenne, for the sake of re-establishing himself as an active U.S.

Marshal and getting an update on things in general and the Driscoll gang specifically.

* * *

Gideon Miles, riding in from the southwest, had arrived in Lusk mere minutes ahead of the Wizarious grand entrance. He'd just hitched his grulla to a rail out front of a saloon called the Thirsty Boot and, with his badge dropped in his pocket for the time being, was getting ready to go inside for a couple drinks to cut the trail dust. The sound of some kind of commotion coming from up the street caused him to pause and look around to see what was going on. Before he could see much, however, his view became blocked by people pouring out of the saloon and other buildings up and down the boardwalk, then crowding close to line the street on either side for the chance to get their own gander and whatever was at hand.

His curiosity getting the better of him, Miles shouldered forward through the pack that had closed around him and claimed his own spot right up front. He could make out a colorful wagon coming down the street and hear the strains of a guitar playing a jaunty tune.

Jammed in beside him was a bare-shouldered Chinese saloon girl in a sequined, short-skirted dress.

"What's going on?" Miles said to her. "Circus or some such rolling in?"

"Nothing quite that good," the girl said in a lilting voice that bore only the slightest hint of an accent. "It's a traveling medicine show that comes around a couple times a year. It's a pretty good one, though, and anything to break the monotony of this tired old town is always welcome."

Miles' gaze followed the approach of the wagons as they rolled closer, stopping every thirty feet or so for the performers to do a little part of their various routines, drawing a round of applause and cheers each time.

As Miles watched the approach of the Wizarious troupe, the saloon girl turned and regarded him more closely. Blacks weren't overly common in and around Lusk. There were five families living within the town limits, and three more struggling to make a go of it on small, outlying farms. Some of the larger cattle ranches in the area also had a handful of black cowboys working for them.

But this fellow here beside her, the saloon girl (she called herself Pearl) concluded, was no dirt farmer or wrangler. His coffee-and-cream complexion was smooth and recently shaved, his hair neatly trimmed, and his clothes, although showing wear and dust from the trail, were good quality and fitted well to his trim build. Plus he had an air of self-assurance—and maybe a hint of danger—about him. No, Pearl decided, this hombre was cut from something quite different and altogether intriguing.

"Although," Pearl said, brushing her right breast against his arm in a manner that, given the crowded conditions, could be taken as either innocent or flirtatious, "not *all* the entertainment we have here in Lusk has to be imported. We also have some very pleasing activities that can be found right here each and every day. Or night."

Miles looked down at her and smiled appreciatively. "Like you, for instance?"

Pearl smiled and pressed both breasts against his arm, this time making the intent very clear. "Well, I really don't like to brag, honey, but …"

"Only, since you're Chinese," Miles pointed out, "doesn't that still make you imported?"

Pearl's smile grew somewhat guarded, unsure if this handsome black man was teasing her, or what he was up to. "The main point," she said, "was that there are ways other than that medicine show to have a good time while you're in town. And—since that show won't go on until this evening—those other things I have in mind are available right away."

Miles put a hand on her bare shoulder. "Well now, pretty lady, you certainly have given me something to consider. And, even though I—"

The show wagons were now rolling by out in the street almost directly before Miles and Pearl. Even as he'd been addressing the young lady, Miles' eyes had been tracking the colorfully staged procession and it was thus that his gaze came to fall on the driver of the second wagon. The sight of this man is what caused Miles to break off in mid sentence. What's more, it caused his jaw to drop and his eyes to bug out to the point where the girl became alarmed he might be having some kind of seizure.

"Are you all right?" she asked with genuine concern.

"I'll be damned!" Miles exclaimed.

"You look like you've seen a ghost."

The show procession was moving past now. The driver of the second wagon had not seen Miles. But Miles continued to gaze after him.

"Little lady," he said to Pearl, "I ain't so sure I just didn't."

–12–

Cash had no trouble finding a pair of candidates who were interested in hiring out to help set up the show. In fact, he had to travel no further than the livery stable just down from where they'd parked the wagons. A couple of strapping, young stable hands there had just finished their chores for the day and, when Cash stopped to inquire if they could recommend anybody, they promptly spoke up for the opportunity to earn some bonus pay for themselves. Cash pointed them toward the wagons, told them to report to the professor, and that matter was taken care of.

As he started away from the stable, Cash began to formulate the wording of the telegram he would soon be sending off to Devon Penn. There was a good chance the chief had worked himself into a near-apoplectic state by now over having not heard from Cash in so long. He might also be worried that something bad could've happened to one of his top marshals (like it did) but he would nevertheless have a store of agitation ready in case there wasn't a good excuse. A corner of Cash's mouth lifted ruefully as he wondered if Penn would consider getting nearly buried alive and then losing his memory an acceptable reason for not reporting in.

"Excuse me, Mr. Famous Show Wagon Driver, sir,

but could I get you to sign an autograph for me?"

Cash had cut around the last corner of the livery building and was headed toward downtown Lusk when the question came out of the shadows of an empty horse stall he had just walked past. The voice was so unexpected that it caused Cash to drop into a half-crouch and spin part way around with his hand streaking to reach for his holstered Colt.

The speaker in the stall, with reasons of his own to be cautious, was also poised with one hand clawed over his gun.

A jolt of recognition froze Cash's hand just as it touched the Colt. His shoulders relaxed and he straightened up from the crouch. "Gideon Miles! By God, man, what a sight for sore eyes you are!"

Miles took a step forward, his body also visibly relaxing. "I might say the same for you, Cash. As a matter of fact, I might say a lot of things where you're concerned. Like, for instance, why the hell hasn't anybody heard a peep out of you for three weeks and more? Don't tell me you gave up marshaling to join some two-bit traveling medicine show?"

Cash couldn't restrain a chuckle. "For the past two weeks, that's sorta been the case. Well, I didn't exactly *join* 'em. It's quite a bit more complicated than that."

Miles cocked an eyebrow. "Oh, I'm pretty sure it's complicated in ways you don't begin to know."

"What's that supposed to mean?" Cash said, his expression sobering.

Miles regarded him. "Sounds like we've both got tales to tell and things to explain. And, I've got a hunch, they might even turn out to be connected in a cockeyed kind of way."

"How so?"

Miles paused for a beat. "What if I was to say I'm in town on the trail of Everett Driscoll and his gang?"

Cash spat a curse. "Those bastards are here?"

"I'm expecting 'em to be, sometime after dark."

"Whatever you got planned for 'em, it goes without saying I'm now part of it."

Miles nodded. "I wouldn't figure anything less. I knew you'd been dogging them back before you seemed to drop off the face of the earth, that's what set me after 'em in the first place."

"Damn near had 'em, too," Cash told him.

"I expect you did, and I'll want to hear the rest of what went wrong." Miles craned his neck, looking around. "But let's find a better place to talk. We've got lots to iron out and not a whole lot of time to do it."

* * *

"In one form or other, I been holdin' the line against lawbreakers for a lot of years," Marshal Ambrose Wick, a stocky man in his middle to late fifties, reflected as he gazed down on the thin puddle of coffee remaining in the tin cup held pressed between his palms. "Rode shotgun for a couple different stage lines. Took turns at bein' a town deputy. Rode my ass off wearin' a county sheriff's star over in Nebraska for a spell. I was back to packin' a deputy's badge when I first came to Lusk. Been the top law dog here for nigh onto six years now."

Wick heaved a ponderous sigh, then lifted his cup

and drained what was left in it. After he'd lowered the cup, he thumb-stroked the curly tips of his rather flamboyant handlebar mustache, making sure the heavily waxed upsweeps hadn't been disturbed.

"Buried two wives along the way," the marshal went on. "Funny, I was the one always facin' down hardcases and dodgin' bullets and the like, yet it was the women in my life who kept kickin' the bucket. Me bein' a persistent cuss, though, I got me a third missus now. She's fifteen years younger than me." A sardonic smile lifted the corners of his broad mouth. "Bein' as how things are so tame and peaceful here in our little town these days, I sorta had it figured it wouldn't be a back or belly full of lead that'd do me in after all. I'd come to reckon it'd more likely be tryin' to keep up with Nora Jean—that's the new missus—in the bed."

Wick paused again and let his gaze slide back and forth between Cash and Miles, who sat across from him at a narrow folding table that had been put up out behind the Wizarious show wagons. Dusk was settling rapidly. Over on the front side of the wagons, the show stage and backdrops were erected and ready, the performers were getting in costume, and a handful of early arrivals were already settling in to claim prime seats.

"Now you two show up," Wick continued gloomily, "to tell me I got the Driscoll gang lurkin' somewhere outside of town, ready to ride in and pay me a visit with some fancy bank-robbin' scheme. Leaves me to fret all over again about checkin' out with my boots on and maybe never makin' it back to my eager young wife again."

"Sorry to bring you a case of the frets, Marshal," said Cash. "But it's the Driscolls fixin' to piss down your well, not us. We're here to help you slap a lid over it."

"Way we got it planned," Miles added, "if we work together, we can catch Everett and his boys by surprise and have the situation bottled up tight before they ever know what hit 'em."

Cash and Miles had repaired to this spot from the livery. After cursory introductions all around, Cash made it clear that he and Miles needed some privacy. Provided that, the two of them then had the chance to update one another on the recent events in their individual experiences that resulted in the fortunate coincidence of arriving in Lusk only minutes apart, both with overlapping goals of bringing down the Driscoll gang.

Cash related how close he'd come to having that task accomplished several days earlier, only to fall short thanks to the untimely rockslide that left him close to death and suffering from memory loss. He told how the Wizarious troupe had saved him and nursed him back to health until his recollection of things started coming back in pieces, culminating with the final part falling into place only the previous night.

For his part, Miles told how Chief Penn had set him on the track of the Driscolls for the double purpose of running them down once and for all and also as a means to hopefully get a line on why Cash—who was known to have been closing in on the gang—suddenly seemed to have disappeared … or joined forces with the outlaws. For the first time, Cash learned how the renown of his name as well as his badge and other personal effects were being put to use in a series of clever ruses that were allowing the gang to hit small town banks and make off with bagfuls of bank money before anybody discovered—not until the banks opened the next morning and the bank president and town sheriff were found locked in the looted vault—what had taken place.

"The lowdown bastards," Cash seethed upon hearing this. "First they leave me for dead, then they try to kill my name and reputation."

"You can thank Chief Penn for playing down those allegations once the reports started coming in," Miles had told him. "I gotta say, though, that 'outlaw marshal' tag you've managed to get attached to yourself over the years didn't exactly help. But the chief and me both refused to believe that, no matter what, you'd ever jump the line to become a bank robber."

"I'm obliged for your belief in me," Cash said earnestly. "I truly am."

Miles had finished up by relating how he'd lucked out by picking up the Driscoll gang's trail following their most recent job and was able to steadily close the gap on them until it was clear Lusk was their next intended target.

With things squared between the two of them, Cash and Miles had agreed it was time to call in the town marshal and lay out the situation for his involvement. Deciding it might be best to try and avoid the three of them being seen confabbing together—just in case—

they'd sent word via one of the short-hire stable hands requesting the mustachioed lawman to join them.

Having now been filled in on the situation, Wick might be outwardly bemoaning the news but at the same time there was a resolve forming in his eyes that left little doubt he could be counted on to help hold the line against Driscoll's bunch.

"What time you figure we can expect ol' Everett and his boys to show up?" he asked.

"The way they've been workin' it," Miles replied, "has been to ride in during or right after the supper hour, when a town's mostly relaxed and starting to settle in for the night. They always go straight to the town marshal's home and start it off with the ersatz Marshal Laramie makin' his pitch about having the Driscolls in custody but bein' badly tuckered out from the trail and wantin' to put 'em in the local lockup overnight so's he can have a chance for some much-needed rest. After that, same spiel for needing a safe place—namely, the bank—for stowin' the robbery money he confiscated and has got with him."

"Pretty slick, gotta give 'em that much," Wick said. "Not hard to see where an unsuspectin' body could fall for it. Fella packin' a U.S. marshal's star rides in herdin' some desperados in cuffs, then reels off a plausible story like that …"

"Yeah, it's slick all right. The town marshals and bank presidents who already fell for it will testify to that."

"What about this show here tonight?" Wick said, indicating the Wizarious wagons and the activity going on beyond them. "Any chance that'll cause a change in plans for the gang? Maybe make 'em hold off until tomorrow night or something?"

"Don't see why," Miles answered. "They'll most likely wait until the show's over and the crowd has thinned and gone home. Might mean they'll show up at your door a little later. Otherwise, I don't see any reason for it to change anything."

"No. I guess not."

"So. Are you willin' to play along with the first leg of it, then?" Cash said to Wick. "Let 'em show up at your place and then take 'em to the jail to supposedly put the 'prisoners' behind bars?"

"I won't do anything to put my wife in danger."

"Goes without saying."

"So I start for the jail with them. Then what? You boys and a couple my deputy are waitin' to waylay us and get the drop on 'em?"

"Close," said Miles. "We're thinking it might be best to get 'em *inside* the jail before we make our move. That way we'll have them boxed in, less risk of one of 'em breakin' away and tryin' to make a run for it."

Wick made a clucking noise with his tongue. "See your point, but it's mighty close quarters in my jail building. Something goes wrong and there's gunplay for any reason, targets won't mean a whole lot—flyin' lead and ricochets could rip hell out of anybody in the room."

"Something goes wrong," Cash pointed out, "you got the same risk of flyin' lead—though not so much ricochets—out in the street, too. A stray round could find an innocent citizen. Plus there'll still be more chance of an opening for one of 'em to try breaking away."

Wick considered. "All right. Six to one, half dozen to the other, I guess." He grinned wryly. "Besides, you two have me outvoted. What's the rest of how you've got it planned?"

–13–

As anticipated, the Driscoll gang didn't put in an appearance until well after the medicine show was over and all spectators had departed and drifted on home to settle in for the night.

The performances had gone well and the crowd response was loud and enthusiastic. Tolos' revised routine—hyped by the professor's dramatic telling (authenticated by the newspaper account he eagerly passed around) of how the strongman had sustained his injury—was a huge hit; and Beatrice's always popular singing and displays of marksmanship also went over big.

Lusk's two saloons had closed while the show was in progress—partly due to expecting they'd have no business during that time anyway, and equally because the proprietors didn't want to miss the acts either. They both opened up again afterward, but for all the customers they drew it was hardly worth the effort.

Ambrose Wick put on the proper display of professional courtesy and eagerness to help a federal officer when Vint, in his role as Deputy U.S. Marshal Cash Laramie, showed up with Everett and the others in chains and under the muzzle of his long-barreled shotgun. Once Vint made his well-practiced pitch,

Wick promptly agreed to house the captured fugitives overnight in his jail. After taking time to strap on his gun belt and send a neighbor boy to ostensibly make sure his deputy would be waiting to assist when they got to the lock-up, Wick led the way through the now-dark streets of Lusk.

The rest of it was set up to go like this:

Wick's deputy, a rather plodding but steady and dependable middle-aged man named Nelson, had been prepped earlier and would be ready at the jail. In addition to the gun he wore on his hip, there was a sawed-off shotgun positioned where it would never be far from his reach.

Cash was also at the jail and ready. In the guise of a rowdy drunk who'd been tossed in the clink earlier, he was clad in ratty, whiskey-soaked clothes and was occupying one of the cells—its door closed but left unlocked. When Wick and the others arrived, he would be lying on the cell's cot, facing away, but in his hands he would be clutching a brace of Colt .44s, prepared to roll and turn in an instant with both guns ready to conduct business.

Miles waited in the deep shadows on the outside of the jail building, armed with his own holstered .44 and a Winchester rifle, poised to spring into action.

The plan was straightforward and simple. Miles was the key, the trigger that would set the final entrapment in motion. The instant Wick and the fraudulent marshal and his prisoners were through the jail house door—before it could be shut and the tables then turned on Wick—Miles and his Winchester would burst in right on their heels to activate quite a contrary turning of the tables. Cash would spring off the cot and out of the cell, Deputy Nelson would swing his sawed-off into play, and Wick would do likewise with his drawn handgun—all aimed to quickly, bloodlessly quell any response or chance for retaliation from the would-be bank robbers.

That was the way it was supposed to go.

But, as is sometimes the way with even the best-laid plan, all it takes is one unexpected misstep to trip up the whole works.

In this instance, literally a misstep resulting in a trip.

When the procession arrived at the jail house, Deputy Nelson was waiting to let them in. He opened the front door and then left it ajar while he stepped back to serve as the inside guard. The prisoners were lined up with Clem in the lead, Burt coming behind him, and Everett bringing up the rear. Vint and his shotgun came along closely behind Everett with Wick at his left side.

Clem stepped up on the narrow strip of boardwalk that ran in front of the jail and moved toward the open doorway. But when Burt lifted his foot to do the same, the toe of his boot caught on the lip of the boardwalk and pitched him off balance. As he started to fall forward, he threw his hands out to catch himself, in the process snapping open the falsely latched handcuffs that were supposed to be restraining him. What was more, when Burt unexpectedly fell against him from behind, Clem, too, was knocked off balance. Reacting with the same instinct, to keep from getting slammed against the door frame, he threw up his hands and his cuffs flew open as well. Further, when he dropped to his knees, the converted Navy Colt pistol Clem had shoved in his waistband, hidden by the fall of his coat, jarred loose and dropped onto the boards with a loud clump.

For a second, everyone seemed to freeze. But with two prisoners unrestrained and a hideaway gun now on display, there could be no pretending that something wasn't seriously amiss.

Wick broke the awkwardly inanimate moment by reaching for the gun on his hip and declaring, "Everybody hold fast! Nobody—"

His command was cut short by Vint, jerking the long barrel of his shotgun around and thrusting it at the lawman. With his sidearm only half drawn, Wick managed to swing his free arm in a desperate, choppy upward motion that knocked the barrel of the gut-shredder skyward just as it discharged with a roar that split the night.

Everybody else was now thrown into frantic activity.

Inside the jail, Deputy Nelson seized up his sawed-off and didn't hesitate to empty both barrels simultaneously into Clem Driscoll as the latter was straightening up in the doorway and reaching for yet another gun under his coat. The double blast lifted Clem off his feet and sent him hurtling backward over the head of the sprawled Burt Ketchel then on out into the dusty street where he rolled lumpy and lifeless between Vint and Everett.

From where he lay, splattered by the hot blood of Clem as he'd passed over, Burt hitched onto one hip and jerked free a handgun from inside his own coat. As

Deputy Nelson was fumbling to thumb reloads back into his sawed-off, Burt shot him in the stomach. When the deputy looked up, his expression one of surprise and dismay, Burt removed all expression from his face by pumping three more slugs into it.

By the time Burt spotted—through the gun powder haze of the sawed-off blast and his own shots—Cash emerging from the inner cell, he had no chance to react. Cash rushed forward, alternately firing both pistols, riddling Burt's head and shoulders until he'd effectively nailed the outlaw to the boardwalk with lead.

Out in the street, Wick had abandoned trying to draw his sidearm and was instead locked in a struggle with Vint, attempting to pry the long-barreled shotgun away from him.

Miles had come around the corner of the jail building with his Winchester raised but unable to find an opening for a clear shot. He gestured with the barrel, shouting, "Get out of the way, Wick! Let me take him."

Meanwhile, Everett Driscoll, seeing the shredded carcass of his brother deposited so coldly and cruelly in the middle of the street, had fallen to his knees beside the remains and became wracked with wailing sobs. He'd jerked free of his handcuff restraints but instead of trying for a gun like the others, he was using his hands to gently cradle Clem's blood-flecked face.

"Everett, God damn you, help me!" shrieked Vint.

When the emotionally shattered gang leader failed to respond to his plea, Vint seemed to react with a surge of desperate rage and at last won the struggle for control of the shotgun. He jerked the weapon free and then immediately lunged with it, slashing the butt savagely across Wick's jaw. The lawman's head snapped back and his body crumpled to the ground.

Continuing the slashing motion that dispatched Wick, Vint used the momentum to fluidly whirl a hundred and eighty degrees. As he came around to face Miles, he dropped into a half-crouch and started to raise the shotgun muzzle.

"Sneaky goddamn double-dealing law dogs!" Vint screamed, his handsome face contorted by near-maniacal fury.

Those turned out to be his last words spoken on earth. A micro-second after Vint shouted them, Miles put a Winchester slug through his heart. Vint's body jerked. He took a shaky backward step but did not fall or drop the shotgun. Although he may have already been dead at that point, he potentially represented too much of a threat to take the chance. Joined by Cash, who had just stepped out of the jail house door with his drawn pistols, Miles chambered a fresh shell and the marshals together finished cutting down the stubborn imposter in a hail of lead.

All of a sudden the street was quiet … except for the continuing ragged sobs of Everett Driscoll.

Cash and Miles approached the man cautiously.

"Don't trust the wily old fox," Cash warned.

"Not about to," Miles assured him.

The pair of marshals moved around behind Everett, keeping their guns trained on him as he remained on his knees in the dirt, continuing to cradle his brother's head in bloodied hands.

"You need to stand up and move away now, Everett," Miles told him calmly. "Keep your hands where we can see them at all times."

Everett seemed not to hear him. He just kept staring down at his brother's blood and dirt smeared face, his broad shoulders still shuddering with heavy sobs.

Miles edged up on one side of him. "It's all over, Everett."

In a hoarse, broken voice, Everett said, "He didn't deserve this … this was going to be our last job … we were going to go to California together."

Cash edged up on the opposite side. His voice was brittle when he spoke. "After you get done dancin' on the end of a rope, you and him will still end up together … burning in Hell."

Everett turned his head slowly and lifted his tear-streaked face. It took a minute but then, even through his grief, recognition sank in. His eyes widened with confusion and a trace of alarm. "You! It can't be … we killed you!"

Cash gazed down at him over the muzzle of the Colt in his right fist. For a long, tense moment it seemed like he might pull the trigger. But then, flatly, emotionlessly, he replied, "Wouldn't you like to think so."

–EPILOGUE–

Cash and Miles left Lusk two days later. Riding between them was a sullen, silent Everett Driscoll. He rode with his head hung low and his wrists once again handcuffed—this time with the bracelets securely locked. On a pack horse trailing behind them were the recovered canvas bags containing the impressive accumulation of stolen bank money.

They left Clem Driscoll, Burt Ketchel, and Vint Brenner behind, buried in the untended Boot Hill corner of the town graveyard.

Deputy Nelson was laid to rest in a more prominent part of the cemetery. There was a large turnout, including Cash and Miles paying their respects.

Ambrose Wick came out of it with a broken jaw, courtesy of Vint's shotgun butt being slammed against it. The town doctor wired it shut, announcing it would take about a month to fully heal and prescribing nothing but a diet of soups and other liquids in the meantime. With Wick's wife—who turned out not only to be young but also very shapely and pretty—constantly fawning over him, he wasn't going to suffer too badly.

"Considerin' that gal's, um, bedside manner and all," Miles commented to Cash on the sly at one point before they left, "you figure there's a chance ol'

Ambrose might not live long enough for his jaw to heal?"

"If it comes to that, it's the way he said he wanted to go, ain't it?" said Cash. Then, with a grim smile, he added, "Beats the hell out of goin' toes up in the middle of a dusty street, you got to give him that."

When the Wizarious show troupe got ready to roll out the day before he and Miles departed, Cash spent a good deal of time saying his farewells to all of them and once again expressing his gratitude for the way they'd cared for him.

Foremost in his farewells, was the one Cash saved for Beatrice when the two of them found a few minutes to be alone together.

"You'll always hold a special place in my heart and memory," he told her sincerely.

She gazed up at him coyly. "Even if you get clunked on the head and lose your memory all over again?"

He kept it serious. "Yes. Even then, I believe."

Beatrice turned serious, too. She reached up and gently slipped her fingers under the arrowhead talisman hanging from a thong around his neck. "It looks just like I imagined," she said in a soft voice. "Where did you find it?"

"The one called Vint was wearing it. Part of his act pretending to be me."

"I'm glad you got it back."

"So am I. Even though I hate the thought of it ever hanging around somebody else's neck."

"What it represents—the love and special bond between you and your mother—can endure that much and more."

Cash met her gaze. He grinned. "Pretty gals like you ain't supposed to be so wise."

"Didn't you know? Some of the greatest minds throughout history have started out singing and shooting in traveling medicine shows."

Beatrice's hand slipped down to the U.S. Marshal badge now pinned on Cash's shirt. She tapped a fingernail against it. "I never really pictured this at all. But, now that I see it on you, it looks exactly right, too. Like it belongs on you."

"You wouldn't have to look very hard to find those who'd argue that point," Cash countered.

Beatrice ran her finger over a fresh nick on one edge of the badge. "Well, maybe those people would feel differently if you took better care of it. This old badge appears the worse for wear. You ought to trade it in for a newer, shinier one when you get back to Cheyenne."

"Vint was wearing that, too. The nick came from one of the slugs me and Miles had to pump into him to put him down."

Beatrice pulled her hand away. "There's an unpleasant image!"

"Yeah, the whole notion of Vint wearing my badge makes for a pretty unpleasant image. Same as with the arrowhead … there's a lot between me and this old badge, too. We've been through plenty together. Too much to forget just because a piece of vermin had his hands on it for a while. It took Miles to make me see that, just like you did a minute ago talking about my arrowhead."

"What did Miles say?"

"He reminded me that a badge on the right man is The Law. Anything else—that same badge lying in a drawer somewhere or pinned to the wrong man—is nothing. Just an empty piece of tin. The man makes the badge, not the other way around. By the same token, the wrong man can't ruin the badge. It just needs to find its way back home."

"You know what I think?" Beatrice said.

"Tell me."

"I think you're a lucky man to be surrounded by so many wise friends."

"I guess I am at that."

"But let me amend something I said a minute ago that, in hind sight, wasn't so wise. When you get back to Cheyenne, don't trade in that nicked up old badge after all. You need it and it needs you … you belong together."

†

–About the Author–

Wayne Dundee lives in the once-notorious old cowtown of Ogallala, on the hinge of Nebraska's panhandle. A widower, retired from a managerial position in the magnetics industry, Dundee now devotes full time to his writing.

To date, Dundee has had nearly a score of novels and novellas plus over thirty short stories published. Much of his work has featured his PI protagonist, Joe Hannibal (celebrating over thirty years on the fictional detective scene and appearing most recently in *Blade of the Tiger*, 2013). He also dabbles in fantasy and straight crime, and lately has done some notable work in the Western genre. His 2010 Western short story, "This Old Star," won a Peacemaker Award from the Western Fictioneers writers' organization. His 2011 novel *Dismal River* won a Peacemaker in the Best First Western Novel category. His 2012 story "Adeline" won a third Peacemaker, again in the short story category.

Titles in the Hannibal series have been translated into several languages and nominated for an Edgar, an Anthony, and six Shamus Awards. Dundee is also the founder and original editor of *Hardboiled Magazine*.

If you enjoyed reading the adventures of Cash Laramie in *The Empty Badge*, you might also like *Manhunter's Mountain* and *The Guns of Vedauwoo*. Or, check out the tales of his grandson, P.I. Jack Laramie, in *Wide Spot in the Road* from the "Drifter Detective" series. All written by Wayne D. Dundee. Available from BEAT to a PULP books at www.beattoapulp.com.

Cash Laramie makes his way down the side of a mountain with a prisoner in tow and two prostitutes eager to flee a mining town that's gone bust, looking to make a new life for themselves. An early winter storm promises to make the journey more than a normal struggle. And, leaving town with two of its most precious gems, the prostitutes, puts Cash in the crosshairs of an angry gang of men who are willing to keep the women in town ... at any cost.

U.S. Marshal Cash Laramie is sent out to locate a shipment of stolen guns in the Vedauwoo area of Wyoming where the rocky terrain is treacherous and enshrouded in mystical beauty. In his quest, Cash goes up against an amoral opportunist looking to stir up discord in the region by selling the weapons to a group of Native Americans.

Vagabond P.I. Jack Laramie stops in the remote town of Buele's Corner for a bite to eat. Before he finishes his bowl of chili, he gets caught up in a tornado of events that starts with a panicked, young couple racing into the diner to use the phone to call for help—a menacing motorcycle gang, The Deguelloes, is chasing after them. When the couple discovers the phone is out of order, Jack steps in to help them fend off the gang who's accusing the couple of running some of their fellow bikers off the road.

Other titles from BEAT to a PULP

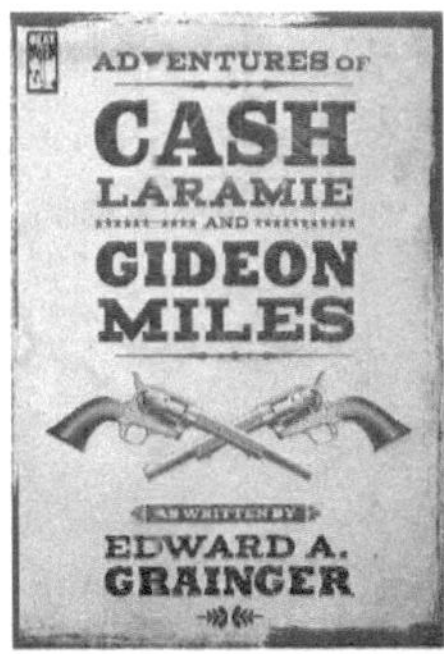

BEAT to a PULP
PO Box 173
Freeville, New York 13068
USA
Email: btapzine@beattoapulp.com
Visit us at www.beattoapulp.com

www.ingramcontent.com/pod-product-compliance
Lightning Source LLC
Chambersburg PA
CBHW032018170626
46807CB00006B/2853
* 9 7 8 0 9 9 0 5 9 1 6 4 1 *